Tales I Grew Up With:

The Grandparents

Tales I Grew Up With:

THE GRANDPARENTS

by Louis F. Badalament, II

Published by Badalament Ink, © 2006

TALES I GREW UP WITH: THE GRANDPARENTS

Edited by Stephanie A. Howse

Book Design by alfeltDESIGN, Oakland, Michigan

Printed by V^2 Printing & Imaging, LLC

Printed in the United States of America

ISBN 978-0-578-00294-1

DEDICATION

Of course, this book is dedicated to every one of my precious grandparents, who were always so generous with their time and tales, but I'd also like to extend a special word of gratitude to everyone else in my family, especially my own dear Mom and Dad.

You're the best.

Grandson's Welcome

You're here!

So glad you were able to make it. Welcome – please, come in! Don't be shy. Make yourself comfortable; my home is your home. Would you care for coffee or a cappuccino… or perhaps just water with a lemon wedge? My Aunt Lisa makes the best creampuffs, and she just dropped some off for you to enjoy. I also have some of my great aunt Moma's Italian cookies. I'll just leave them out here on this plate for you to enjoy.

Now, I understand you've come to hear me tell the tales I grew up with. Just so that you understand, these stories were collected from all four of my grandparents. Storytelling plays a big role in my family. Practically every time we get together, my grandparents will roll out one of their old household stories that have become so familiar to me, but never stale, even after all these years. Then one day, I stumbled upon a notion – Why not pass them on to others? – and they agreed that I could go ahead and share them with you.

The tales, themselves, are of a wide and well-mixed variety. Some are unique to our family – personal accounts from the grandparents' own lives, or older history dating even before their *time. Others are flat-out fables… parables to illustrate and entertain in the style of Aesop. Fact or fable, each tale should be regarded as its own stand-alone story, complete with its own beginning, middle and end. Bear in mind, also, that these tales weren't all handed to me in a single day; they were given out to me, one at a time over many years, when it was appropriate to tell it, when they felt I needed to hear it, to drive a lesson home.*

Now that's said, let's sit down and enjoy the coffee, cookies and creampuffs and we can get started…

Table Of Contents

Part I

Grandma Badalament

Father's Mother

Meet Grace Costello Badalament

Grace Costello was the second-youngest child in a family of seven children, the daughter of impoverished Italian immigrants. Her father was a factory worker and laborer, while her mother was a homemaker. Grace's family was so poor, her mother used to make bread for the family because they could not afford to buy their own loaves. Driven by a burning love for the craft, Grace studied dance under her own steam with passionate zeal, and landed the break of her life at age eleven; a seven-year contract with MGM studios.

Her formative years were spent dancing for Hollywood; she virtually supported her whole family from her MGM salary, performing specialty parts involving dance forms such as tap, ballet, flamenco and ballroom dancing. She performed in Pantages and Orpheum Theaters. She went to school at MGM studio with the Our Gang kids, taking lessons in drama, elocution, and dance alongside Virginia Wiedler, Elizabeth Taylor, and Mickey Rooney. She met Clark Gable, Robert Taylor, Hedy Lamar, Maureen O'Hara, Lana Turner, Robert Preston, Eleanor Pow-

ell, Fred Astaire, Cyd Charisse, Judy Garland, Jimmy Stewart, Spencer Tracy, Katharine Hepburn and many, many more.

While under contract, Grandma was shielded from the seedier side of show business by virtue of her minor status; by law she was accompanied by her mother. However, at the end of her seven-year contract, Grandma was a young woman of eighteen. She could have stayed on as an actress and a dancer, but the allure of the cinema had dimmed for her. She knew that further advancement at Hollywood would almost certainly mean compromising many things she held near and dear to her heart.

So she left the entertainment industry altogether, met and married my Grandfather, Louis Badalament, and became a stay-at-home mom. Together, they had six children, including my father, Robert. When asked, Grandma told me that she was glad of the time she spent working at MGM studios, that she had fun and it taught her a great deal… but she never regrets her decision to leave Hollywood.

Quotes She Lived By

- *"Money and power are the world's greatest deodorant."*
- *"Only the boring get bored."*
- *"We are three things. What we think we are. What others think we are. And what God truly knows us to be."*
- *"No man lacks the inclination, only the opportunity."*
- *"Wrong is wrong, even though everyone's doing it. Right is right, even when nobody's doing it."*
- *"A drop of oil, placed in water, always rises to the top."*
- *"A good mother takes care of herself, otherwise she cannot take care of her children."*
- *"Pray as though everything depends on God; work as though everything depends on you."*
- *"When a fish stinks, it starts at its head."*
- *"Don't spit at the sky, or it'll land back on your face."*
- *"He who hoots with the owls at night cannot soar with the eagles in the morning."*
- *"Don't try to fool me, I'm your mother! I put those hairs on your head!"*

Chapter One

Gotta Dance!

If you were lucky enough to have been living in Michigan in the year of 1936, and had happened to be strolling the streets of Dearborn on an early weekday morning, there is a good chance that a very unusual girl had passed you by on her way to school.

This girl's name was Grace Costello. She was all of eight years old; dark-haired, fair-skinned, cute as a button. Yet, it would never have been her looks drawing your attention upon her. On a fine morning like this, with the ground so dry and un-slippery, Grace's slender feet would have been *all over the place*.

Over sidewalks, onto ledges, twirling circles in midair! With so much energy yet to be spent, little Grace would never set forth in such a boring way as *walking*! No; the girl's toes would tap back and forth, side to side, her heels brushing back upon the pavement in measured tempo. Her whole body would spin about in half-turns and full-circles, swinging her hips with a flair that could only be pure vaudeville, not even seeing you as she leaped forward with a stylish series of high kicks.

Obviously, this was a girl who did not really care about actually *reaching* her destination. Whatever stares or snickers she would draw, Grace was quite happy sweeping about to music only she could hear, losing herself completely to the pure exhilaration of dance.

Much happier than she was having to put up with *school*. What a supreme load of garbage! For five days of every week, Grace had to plant herself at her stupid Miller School desk in Dearborn, Michigan, and force herself to remain in her seat – for *six whole hours* with just a *measly* little lunch break in between! – while boring old Mrs. Peterson rattled on about stupid stuff Grace knew she'd never use!

Gotta Dance!

"A noun is a person, place, or thing," Mrs. Peterson would say, scratching it onto the great chalkboard on the wall behind her, "'Mary' is a noun… 'America' is a noun... and 'candy' is a noun."

"Is 'dancing' a noun?" Grace had asked, on one of the few instances she'd bothered raising her hand.

"'Dancing' is more of a *verb*," Mrs. Peterson told her, "Although… depending on how you were using it, 'dancing' *could* be a noun... like if you were taking 'Dancing' as a class in school."

Too bad they taught no such class in Miller School! Grace had been very sour that night at her kitchen table, doing writing homework.

"This is nice… like I can *write*!" Grace grumbled, wearing out her brain trying to sort verbs from nouns when her own *teacher* couldn't give her a straight answer on the subject! "What am I wasting my time here for?"

Reading and writing were for frail little librarians, anyway, not prima ballerinas like her!

And if Grace hated writing, she absolutely *loathed* mathematics.

"Grace, what does nine plus nine equal?" Mrs.

Peterson asked one morning, startling her out from Gene Kelly daydreams.

"Nineteen?" Grace tried, uncertainly.

"Close – *eighteen*." Grace's cheeks burned with embarrassment as the twenty-nine other girls in her class giggled around her.

"Here I am, wasting my whole life trying to do math that I'm too stupid to do!" Grace muttered to herself, returning home that afternoon – not prancing and cavorting as she had on her way down, but dragging her feet through the dust.

That was when the little dancer decided things were going to change. She had *ambitions*, Grace did, and they did *not* involve idiotic busywork like the kind Mrs. Peterson put her through!

That next morning, Grace took two special pairs of shoes from her bedroom closet and placed them in their own separate bag. These were her toe shoes – which were for practicing ballet – and her tap shoes – which had Supertone taps screwed on their soles for the *clickety-clack* sound in tap-dancing. She got to Miller School early, in a straight-out run this time, and crept downstairs to the basement gym, hiding her bag of shoes in one of the lockers. Several minutes af-

ter Mrs. Peterson's class went in session, Grace raised her hand.

"I'm not feeling well," she informed her teacher. "My head feels all woozy, and strange purple spots are flashing in my eyes. And I think I feel a bloody nose coming on, too."

"Why don't you go down to the gym and lie on one of the cots until you feel better?" Grace knew Mrs. Peterson would tell her this, because she had fallen sick in her class once before.

Now excused, Grace hurried down to the basement. She had the whole gymnasium to herself, now… gym classes wouldn't start until eleven o'clock. Grace took her shoes out from the locker and set them to good use. She danced her little heart out: *pliés*, pirouettes, and the whip-snap *fouettés* of ballet! The snazzy styles of tap: the Charleston, Black Bottom, and the smooth Bombershay! In class, Grace was nothing but a bored little schoolgirl, going through the motions. Here, Grace was the star of her own private show, smack-dab in center-stage limelight!

Oh, it was a dream beyond imagining! So lost was Grace in her own glorious fantasy, that she didn't even see the gym teacher enter into the room. She had come in to check on some equipment, and found Grace poised with one leg stretched straight-back, and an arm stretched straight-forward in a magnificent *arabesque*. The gym teacher didn't stop the 'sick' little girl, or call out to her, but closed the door quietly, and went straight to the girl's homeroom teacher.

Grace returned to her classroom after what she felt was an appropriate length of time.

"Feeling better, Grace?" Mrs. Peterson asked, by way of welcome. "You look a little flushed."

"I'll be fine!" Grace assured the woman.

Mrs. Peterson shrugged, and her lessons resumed in their usual manner. Grace let the words wash over her without really absorbing any of it. At last, the end-of-school bell rang, and everybody scrambled under their desks to grab their bags.

"Oh, Grace?" Mrs. Peterson called out, "I don't want you going home just now. I need to speak to you." Grace stiffened, for the first time wondering whether her little ploy might've hit a snag.

The classroom emptied until it was just she and her teacher, alone in this room. Grace had sat back down, alert as a cornered squirrel. The teacher rose up, wiping the last of today's lessons off the chalkboard.

"You know, Grace, I *admire* your ambition. You want to be a dancer… and I think you're going to really be *something*, someday." Grace sparkled at the compliment, but the teacher stopped erasing and looked over her shoulder. "But I'm afraid for you, too, because everybody's going to make a fool of you."

Until this point, Grace had not trusted herself to speak. Now the little dancer sputtered, "*No one's* going to make a fool of me!"

"Oh, but they'll *have* to," Mrs. Peterson countered, not unpleasantly. "You're a girl who can't add, subtract, or divide. When they ask you about money, you won't understand because you don't know math. When they give you a contract to read, you'll be too stupid to understand."

Mrs. Peterson turned from her chalkboard and sat at a desk – not the big teacher's desk at the front of the room, but a student's desk, right by Grace. "In a contract, if one little word, "*if*" is in there, it'll change the whole complexion of the contract. You could become a servant, without being paid, for many years, because you are not educated."

Grace couldn't meet the older woman's eyes. Mrs. Peterson sighed.

"You will be rubbing elbows with big stars… who do you love?"

Grace's eyes misted over. "Fred Astaire! Eleanor Powell!"

The teacher nodded. "You'll be out chatting with them, and they'll be speaking beautiful English; deep thoughts that have nothing to do with dancing. And there you are… with such inadequate verbal skills. You'll come across as stupid. And you'll feel cheap."

Grace flinched in her chair, as though Mrs. Peterson had brandished a whip. The truth was, Grace wasn't from a wealthy family, and they wouldn't be *getting* wealthy anytime soon. Unless *somebody* big could recognize her talents and she finally got her big break…

As if reading these thoughts, Mrs. Peterson continued, "You have to be more than a good dancer to be a star; you have to be educated enough to manage your success."

Fire flashed in Grace's eyes. "I *will* be a star!" she asserted, as though her name was flashing in Broadway lights already.

“Then you’d better do this,” Mrs. Peterson said, with a nod to Grace’s schoolbooks, “and be prepared.”

Then Mrs. Peterson stood up and left the classroom herself, without a further word to Grace. That afternoon, Grace did not dance her way back home, but she didn’t drag her feet, either. She walked, like a normal little girl, full of thoughts that kept bumping into each other as she went.

Grandma Badalament - Father’s Mother

Chapter Two

Filled to the Brim

Young Grace Costello was sitting at her living room window one afternoon after school, thinking about happiness—not so much her own personal happiness, as happiness in general. Everything everyone did in life seemed aimed at getting happy, or staying happy. It came as effortlessly as smiling for some, while other folks spent their whole lives scrambling for any elusive scrap of contentment with nothing to show for it at the end.

Filled to the Brim

Grace pondered, and she philosophized, and when she had explored the matter from every angle she could think of, she went into the kitchen to get her mother's take on the subject. She found Mrs. Costello chopping onions by the sink.

"Mom," Grace asked, seating herself at the table, "why is it that someone who's poor can still be happy?"

The percussive *thump-thump-thump* of the chopping stopped, and the mother peered over at her daughter. The two of them were working hard to pull themselves from poverty, so she was unsure how to interpret this question.

"I just wanted to hear your thoughts on it," Grace explained.

Her mother said nothing at first, turning back to her sink. But then she picked three items from around her, and brought them to the tabletop.

A thimble, a cup, and a big pitcher full of lemonade.

"Fill the cup." Mrs. Costello said.

Grace took the pitcher and poured enough lemonade so that the cup was almost full.

"All the way," her mother corrected.

Grace almost argued, but chose instead to carefully pour enough lemonade to pool precariously around the cup's rim—one or two drops away from a sticky mess.

Next, her mother pushed the thimble forward.

"Now fill this up, just as much."

The thimble was such a tiny thing, Grace couldn't even fit her pinky finger into it, but she tilted the pitcher so that just enough drops slid inside without the thimble running over.

"Grace," her mother chided, "*just as much* means pour exactly the same amount of lemonade into the thimble as you poured into the cup."

"But it'll spill all over everything!" Grace protested. "The thimble is at least twenty times smaller than the cup!"

"And that's the way some people are," her mother said, smiling. "Each person decides on their own just how much it takes for them to feel fulfilled. *That's* how the poor can find happiness."

With that, Grace's mother took the thimble, raised it like a toast, and sipped it down.

Chapter Three

Grace's Big Break

Since her talk with Mrs. Peterson, Grace had become a very avid reader of books, but dancing always remained her first passion. The older she got, the better she danced, and there came a day when the Costello family grew so impressed by her talent that they decided to leave Michigan and move all the way down to California, to improve Grace's chances of attracting some professional attention.

Grace was heading home from school one morning, when something nailed to a telephone pole caught her eye. It was a poster for a Hollywood audition session that would be taking place this coming Thursday. Grace's excitement grew as she read they were looking for dancing girls! She hustled home, and announced the news to her mother and father.

"They're having auditions down at the corner of Garnet and Santa Ana on Thursday!"

"When, Grace?" asked Mrs. Costello, her mother.

"Nine to five," Grace replied.

"Don't you have school then?"

Grace's face fell momentarily. But then she shrugged, said, 'Oh well,' and went to her room to get started on her homework. While she certainly wasn't about to give up on dancing, Grace was eleven, now… and had grown up enough to put her schoolgirl's responsibilities ahead of her wishful dreams.

Mr. Costello, however, had other designs in mind. On Thursday morning, about half an hour earlier than when she was normally roused from bed, Grace found herself being shaken awake by her father.

"Don't tell your mother," Mr. Costello said, in a low, quick whisper, "Hide your tap shoes and such in your bag, the way you did that one time back in Michigan. Pretend that you're going to school, but head to that audition that's taking place today, instead."

"All alone?" Grace asked, eyes widening.

"You're going to do it!" said Mr. Costello, in his usual domineering manner. "You go in there!"

What else could Grace do? So she stowed everything she'd need into her schoolbag, kissed her mother goodbye, and set out for the studio on the corner of Garnet and Santa Ana. Even though it was still fairly early in the morning when Grace arrived, a long line of girls had already formed ahead of her, stretching out the studio's front doors and around the opposite corner of the Santa Ana boulevard. Glumly, she wound her way around them, taking her place at the end of the line.

What she could see of the aspiring hopefuls ahead of her did nothing to inspire her confidence. She saw curtains of hair, elegantly styled in curves and waves, and cheeks glistening from professional makeup. They had come in dazzling costumes, frills and lace and shiny new shoes bought just for the occasion. The Costello family was very poor, and Grace had only two dresses to her name: the one she was wearing, and the one in her mother's wash – she was forever alternating between the two.

It wasn't just the swarm of pretty faces which worried Grace – a lot of the other girls had come accompanied by their parents, their agents... even their dance instructors! She could see them desperately rehearsing the turns and transitional steps in their dance routines, warming-up with stomach-tightening contractions and pivot turns.

'*I can't do it!*' she despaired to herself inwardly. '*I can't win!*'

But she knew how dreadfully upset her father would be if she chickened out and retreated back home or off to school, so for his sake, she remained in line. The queue advanced sluggishly, none of the girls bothering to talk to one another. Hopeless as it all seemed, Grace never stepped out of line. Competition would be fierce, Grace knew, as more girls yet joined in line behind her. Occasionally, a rejected applicant would sweep past Grace, receiving consolation from the members of her entourage.

Time ticked along, and the sun began to fall. She was now almost inside the building when a frumpy woman who didn't look like anyone's mother stepped out from the studio's doors.

"We're sorry," she shouted out, "But auditions are officially over." Grace saw girls in front and behind her sobbing and grumbling, even screaming in fury as they strode away, but she didn't move.

The frumpy woman hadn't bothered to lock the doors. Grace waited for the streets to clear, then snuck inside, stealing through the hallways until she arrived at what looked like the right office. Through a partially-opened door, Grace spotted the frumpy woman filing papers at a desk. She fell back out of sight, seizing her opportunity when the secretary stepped out for a bathroom break. She crept in and slipped through the important-looking door beyond the secretary's desk.

It seemed to Grace that the secretary's boss had already gone home as well. Behind the office desk, there was nothing to see but an imposing chair, facing the side window. Suddenly, it swiveled around to face her. A little man, just slightly taller than Grace, herself, fixed Grace with a frank stare. His teeth were clenching a truly impressive cigar, as long as a maestro's baton. Her eyes darted to the nameplate on the edge of his desk – Edward Small.

"Don't call your secretary, Mr. Small!" Grace implored. Her tongue felt like leather in her mouth, yet her voice was strong. "I want you to watch and listen to me, and just tell me the truth. You *can* tell me the truth, can't you? You won't lie to me?"

"What are you doing here?" the man asked. No trace of alarm or anger carried in his voice.

"I want you to tell me if I have talent," Grace answered, easing out of her walking shoes and emptying things from her bag. "And if I haven't… be honest and I'll go back home. Because we're very poor, and we have to pay our bills, and they're going to turn off our electricity tomorrow."

Her tap shoes weren't the only thing she'd snuck past her mother that morning; there was also a tap board, a record, and a little Victrola to play it on. Rich strands of smoke coiled around Small's face as Grace set herself up, unrolling the tap board and setting the Victrola in a chair intended for Small's visitors. Nervous all the while, she still continued to talk. "They're going to turn off our gas, our lights… but if *you tell me* that I have talent…"

"What will you do?" Edward Small interrupted.

Confidence washed over Grace; it was all-or-nothing now. "I'm not going to quit. I was going to tell you I was, but *I know* I have talent. I just want to hear you say it, because you're a big man."

And he was – in the film industry, if not in stature. Small started his talent agency in the 1920's, co-founded two short-lived movie studios, and produced many timeless Hollywood classics including *The Count of Monte Cristo*, *The Man in the Iron Mask*, and *My Son, My Son*.

"Go ahead," said Mr. Small.

She started the Victrola up with a twist of the crank, centered herself on the tap board, and performed, right in his office.

She started off with a soft-shoe number, shuffling her feet to Duke Ellington's 'Sophisticated Lady,' then moved on to the faster grooves of 'Sheik of Araby,' dancing with the full skill of her years. Edward Small followed her every shift and pivot with eyes that never widened with delight nor creased in distaste, but kept attentive, gauging. It was rather like performing for someone's stogie-smoking cat.

Once the number had ended, Mr. Small told her, "I want you. Be at MGM at nine o'clock, tomorrow morning. I'm going to make a session of auditions, and I want people to see you perform. And if they say what

I think they will… you're going to have a seven-year contract."

"Really?" asked Grace, willing herself to hold calm. "You're not fooling me?"

"No," said Mr. Small, handing her his business card. "I want to be your agent."

She shook his hand gratefully, turning to go.

"Incidentally, you're broke?" Mr. Small added, stopping her with his voice.

"Yes," said Grace.

Small dug in his pockets, producing a big wad of money. "This is for your performance today," he told her. "Personality is a commodity, and you have it."

She counted out a couple of hundred dollars.

"God bless you," she said, to which Mr. Small replied, "He does."

It was late when Grace returned home, and she was quickly cornered by her mother. "What did you do?!" Mrs. Costello demanded. When Grace showed her the money, she paled.

"What's going on?!" she gasped, moaning in Italian while biting her fingers, imagining every possible criminal act.

Grace handed her Mr. Small's business card. "Here's the man's card. My ship is *in*. We're going to be *famous*!"

From nine until five that next day at MGM, Grace had nothing to eat. Hollywood hotshots shuffled in and out to watch her dance among various groups of professionals.

But she got the contract.

Chapter Four

Paycheck Payback Payoff

At fourteen years old, Grace Costello was well established within the daily grind of showbiz. Although she had been performing for MGM studios for quite some time, she had never been cast in a noteworthy role. Grace was one bloom in a bouquet of dancing girls, moving from costume to costume, and from show to show. Other actresses might have been disheartened to find themselves stuck with bit roles for so many years, but not Grace.

She was content. Her career was demanding enough as a nameless extra, with lessons to attend, choreography to rehearse, and hours performing on stage. It was steady work doing what she loved, and she was making money – five hundred dollars a week, with the lion's share going straight to her family back home.

One particular payday, around noon, Grace was handed her check in the usual manner. She flipped it against a wall and signed the back before heading to lunch. Then it was off to the wardrobe department for a fitting of new tutus, yoga instruction, and more rehearsals. Just when the director had called it a day and the company was packing up their things, Grace felt for her paycheck, and found it was missing.

Panic welled up inside her as she flew through the dressing room, searching. She flung open lockers, questioned friends and strangers, hunted through rooms she knew she'd never even been in on the off chance that her paycheck would somehow be there… but to no avail. Whoever had it, wherever it was, it was gone for good. So distraught was Grace, so frustrated with herself that she sat down crying like her heart would break.

Quite suddenly, she felt a little tap on her shoulder. Pulling her hands from her eyes, Grace caught her reflection gleaming back at her from a glossy pair of black Oxford shoes, covered with spats. She looked up and saw a man standing in front of her – handsome, long-faced, clean-shaven and excellently groomed. This fellow was an actor by the name of Vittorio De Sica. Grace recognized him instantly. De Sica was an accomplished veteran of his craft who had starred in many acclaimed films. In time, De Sica would land the part of Major Alessandro Rinaldi in a 1957 adaptation of *A Farewell To Arms*, acting alongside such theatrical greats as Rock Hudson and Sophia Loren.

Now, however, was the first time De Sica and Grace had met, and the last time they would ever speak. De Sica always went with a cane in his hand, though he wasn't in any way crippled. He just liked the effect of it.

"You mustn't *cry*," De Sica spoke at last, "as if the world is coming to an end."

Resentment fluttered within Grace as she stared back at his cap – one end tilted up just so. "Not for you," she told him, "You have a lot of money. My little check doesn't mean anything to you, but it means a lot to my family, and I lost it to my stupidity!" She was sobbing too hard to say anything else, so she just hid her face again, hoping the older man would leave her to her misery.

"You signed it?" questioned De Sica, as he bent down towards Grace.

Grace nodded.

"That *was* stupid," De Sica agreed. "You should have signed it at the teller's."

"I *know*!" Grace howled through her tears.

Vittorio De Sica sighed, flexing his grip on the cane he carried everywhere – as though it were a prop for a tap-dancing number they'd all be breaking into any moment now.

"If you stop crying, I'll tell you what you can do to rectify this, but you have to listen." Grace looked up at him, holding her sniffles in. "Never cry over anything that can't cry over you." De Sica paused a beat. "Did you hear that? I'll repeat it... never cry over *anything* that doesn't cry over you."

She swallowed, offering him a weak smile. He plucked a silken handkerchief from his corner pocket and dabbed at her eyes.

"Now I'm going to tell you how you can get your money," De Sica said, helping Grace to stand, "Go to

Mr. Mayer…"

"Mr. *Mayer?*" Grace squeaked. The Mayer they were referring to, of course, was none other than the iconic founder… *the* Mayer of Metro-Goldwyn-Mayer. "What would I say?!"

"Tell him the truth, as you told me." De Sica advised her, "I think Mr. Mayer will know what to do."

He turned then, and strode away at a debonair gait; no English dandy could have made a more dapper man-about-town. When her tears had stopped flowing, and she had gotten hold of herself, Grace set out and found the office of Louis B. Mayer. She peeked inside, and saw there were several businessmen talking with him. She closed the door gently, but Mayer had already spotted her.

"What is it?" he called out.

She edged into his office, clutching the doorknob at her back. "This is very, very confidential," she told him, quietly.

Mayer looked at her, then turned towards the other men there. "Well, the young lady has something to tell me. Why don't you guys go into the other room?"

So they did, without complaint.

Paycheck Payback Payoff

Grace had never known stage fright quite like this. If the studio had caught fire, at least there'd be an *excuse* for her being here... but to interrupt a meeting and perhaps risk losing her *job* over a stupid week's *salary*?

"Mr. Mayer, I'm in trouble." she started. " I don't know what you can do to help me, but I need to have the amount of my check reimbursed, and..." her mind worked furiously, "I will pay you ten dollars out of my salary every week until we're square." She waited for the axe to drop.

"Can I trust you?" Mayer asked her, seriously.

"Oh, yes. I'm very honorable." Grace assured him. "I wouldn't cheat you, you're my *boss*!"

She watched Mayer open his pockets and take out the money she needed.

"Um... do you want me to sign anything?" Grace asked. Practically every time money traded hands with Louis Mayer, a contract was sure to creep up.

"No," said Mayer, "I think I can trust you."

Every week for the next year, whenever Grace got her paycheck, she would stop in Mayer's office and personally relinquish ten dollars to the millionaire movie mogul. On the day the debt was completely paid off, Mayer called her back into his office and led her to his desk. Opening a drawer, he took out a bankbook.

"This is for you," he informed her.

"For what?" Grace asked, frowning slightly.

"You were honest," Mayer told her, with the warm appreciation of someone who doesn't see such things everyday, "so I opened up an account for you, and I put all that money in it."

Grace looked in the bankbook to find five hundred dollars written in her account. She was so thrilled, she completely forgot herself and started to cry.

Chapter Five

MGM and Their Majesties

It was the summer of 1941. Franklin D. Roosevelt was enjoying his third term of presidency in Washington D.C., Hitler's Nazis were laying siege across Europe, and George VI reigned as King of Great Britain and Ireland. Regrettably, His Majesty didn't get out of London much. England was struggling against the Third Reich, and King George was struggling against lung cancer brought on by a smoking habit. His daughter Elizabeth, though, could still afford to travel abroad. She was young and in love – eager for a chance to distance herself from her homeland's ordeals for awhile. Accompanied by her fiancé, Philip Mountbatten, Princess Elizabeth took a plane out to the United States. MGM Studios couldn't believe its luck when the royal couple phoned in to say they'd be paying a visit.

Grace Costello was twelve at this time. The prospect of entertaining honest-to-goodness British royalty held her in a flurry of giddy anticipation and fretful nerves – and she wasn't the only one. Everyone from the chief executives down to the broom pushers were yanking all the stops out to ensure that Elizabeth's stay would be the most fun and memorable Hollywood could produce. The top brass were actually a little apprehensive, in truth. Elizabeth's call had come on such short notice, when a fair percentage of their biggest stars were out-of-town, enjoying their own summer vacations. Still, enough celebrities were at hand that even the heiress presumptive of England's throne shouldn't feel cheated out of a fun time.

When Elizabeth and Philip finally arrived, Louis Mayer and Samuel Goldwyn, themselves, were there to welcome them. It was fantastic publicity for their studio, with journalists and cameramen from both sides of the pond snapping photos of the princess and her consort shaking hands with the moviemakers. Their royal guest spent most of her day on a grand tour of MGM studios, with Mr. Mayer acting as guide.

He showed Elizabeth the sound sets where the film soundtracks were recorded and the backstage rooms where actors and actresses had their makeup applied while waiting for their scenes. They watched costumes being threaded together by the designers of the wardrobe departments, and carpenters piece together sets for future movies.

She and Philip traded small talk with the likes of Judy Garland, Mickey Rooney, and Roddy McDowell. Mayer showed them the splendor of Tara, as seen in *Gone With The Wind*, Father Flanagan's orphanage from *Boys Town*, and the vine-strewn jungle boughs where Tarzan had pounded his chest and belted out his classic ape scream.

Throughout the day, Grace found all sorts of excuses to dash off to wherever Elizabeth and Philip happened to be, just to look at them. She'd have loved a chance to speak with them directly, but wherever they went, Elizabeth and Philip were escorted by a small squad of bodyguards, all skilled at insulating their princess from the general public. Still, from what

Grace observed of them, they were truly a credit to their country. Princess Elizabeth was fifteen, just a few years older than herself. It impressed Grace how sweet and well-mannered both she and Philip were – nothing arrogant about them. They were appreciative and grateful to everyone in MGM for this lovely treat.

*They're the real thing...*Grace thought to herself, *they don't fake it the way some people do.*

Later that evening, Grace was to be found backstage, in the company of thirty-five dancing girls who would be sashaying out to put on a little after-dinner floor show for Elizabeth II and her future husband. The bodysuits they wore had been fashioned to emulate men's eveningwear, with sequined coattails at their backs, flashy bowties at their collars, and dainty top hats on their heads.

Grace was near the brink of honest fear. She stood with her back against the wall, smiling rigidly at every passerby, frantically dredging up the confidence she'd need to perform before the curtain rose. She could do this. It was just a simple tap-dancing routine they'd rehearsed and re-rehearsed, with a tiny bit of singing. She *wouldn't* freeze up and forget the whole act just because the future King and Queen of England were out there.

"Hey, Grace." The man who'd stopped in front of her was Richard Greene, a handsome English heart-throb, who had starred in *Hound of the Baskervilles*, and later would become famous in the TV series *Robin Hood*. Greene was the main feature in this act, Grace and the other dancers serving as chorus line to his singing and dancing. "Nervous?"

"I'm trying *not* to be," she told him, "I *should* be alright in a few minutes."

Greene let out a breath. "Their Royal Highnesses got you spooked?"

"A little." she admitted.

Greene bent down so they were eye-level. "Remember, Grace... they have to go to the bathroom just like everybody else."

Grace gawked... and laughed. What had gotten into her? She hadn't been this star-struck since before she'd started dancing for MGM. She'd been intimated then, too... by the stars, by the audiences, by the whole pomp and circumstance of showbiz. But after the first six months, Grace had stopped regarding the actors as some higher form of humanity.

"Thanks." she said, feeling refreshed.

"Chin up, kid." Greene said, walking away.

"Break a leg, Mr. Greene." she called after him, taking her place in the chorus line.

The orchestra pit sprang to life with a blare of trumpet fanfare, the music building to a swinging, jazzy overture. The great red curtain flew upward, disappearing into darkness as Grace Costello, with a big smile on her face, stepped out to dance.

Chapter Six

No Questions Asked

This is an old story my Great Grandma Costello used to tell her daughter, Grace. Grandma Badalament, in turn, passed it down to us.

• • •

The year was 1907, and a father had died, leaving behind his widowed wife and their six-year-old son, Fabrizio. Fabrizio's family had never been well-to-do to begin with, but his father had left behind nothing but debt... and his mother could barely make ends meet with the pittance she got sweeping floors at the tavern. The two of them lived together in a tumbledown shack, somewhere in a small Italian village of no particular distinction.

"Oh, what are we ever to do?!" Fabrizio's mother would wail. Oftentimes, the woman would go hungry so her boy could eat, and Fabrizio would listen to her stomach rumbling all through the night. It was a dismal existence – their clothes were threadbare, they had nowhere to go, and Fabrizio's mother wasn't getting any younger.

It came to pass, one afternoon, as the mother returned home from her miserable job, she found her son standing in the center of the room, looking strangely anxious.

"Um... here, Mama," he said, bringing his hands from around his back. "This is for us."

He was holding an apple out for her – fresh, crisp, and untouched with spots. Oh, was the mother ever happy! "Fabrizio, you are so thoughtful!" she trilled, and hunted through her paltry stack of belongings until she'd found her knife. She cut the apple in half, and together, mother and son enjoyed the fruit.

The day after that, the shack was empty when

the mother returned home, but Fabrizio wasn't long in coming. Not a full hour later, the little boy was rapping on the door, pockets sagging with two pears. She hugged him dearly, and darted back inside, meaning to fetch the knife.

"Don't bother, Mama," Fabrizio called after her. "Eat it all yourself, it's alright… I've eaten already."

Indeed, the boy's stomach sat a bit fuller than usual. Joyful tears spilled down her cheeks as the juice trickled to her chin.

The third morning was a veritable feast – onions, potatoes, and bunches of grapes. The mother was thrilled to death, kissing Fabrizio all over, saying, "My son, you are the savior of this family!"

Thus, a routine was established in their little household. Fabrizio and his mother would go their separate ways in the morning, and Fabrizio would return with great bounties to share. Now, you might be wondering… how was such a young boy coming by such provisions? Did he work in the fields? Did he dance on a stage? Did he go out into the woods and forage for it, like the nomadic hunters of time gone by?

The strange truth was… the matter was never addressed. For Fabrizio's mother, it was enough that her wonderful, caring, resourceful, loving little boy was bringing in these magnificent gifts for her needy self… the details always seemed to work themselves out well enough, after all. As for Fabrizio… well, since his mother never seemed to trouble *her* head about it, he saw no reason to broach the subject, himself.

The years rolled on, and as Fabrizio grew older, he kept bringing home more and more. When Fabrizio was thirteen, he turned out his pockets so that a small shower of coins tumbled into his mother's lap.

"My God!" she cried, plucking them out of her apron, "You're better than your father!"

To be certain, Fabrizio didn't fork *everything* he brought home over to his mother, but he always took care to give her some *portion* of it. On and on it went, and she praised Fabrizio endlessly, in every way she knew how – he never asked for anything more than that. When Fabrizio turned eighteen, he led his mother out of the grubby shack they'd lived in so long and ushered her into a horse-drawn carriage. When the horses stopped, they were standing before a freshly painted two-story house with a garden, chickens, and a cobbled path leading to the front porch.

"This," said Fabrizio, "is our new home."

Heaven itself couldn't have made the mother happier. She had all the food she could eat, beautiful clothes on her back, and a fine house she could be proud to show off. In time, Fabrizio was even able to hire an attendant to see to her every need. She was as happy as any woman could ever be, and would have been wholly content for life to continue like this until the end of her days.

The year was 1921 when finally, Fabrizio was caught. Only here, when the authorities had brought his case to trial, were the details of Fabrizio's sordid career brought fully to light. Fabrizio had never held a legitimate job in his life. He stole. Even his new house had been purchased with stolen money.

He had been very clever about it all these years, but the police had cornered him with a pearl necklace belonging to the wife of an old army colonel, and evidence of older, forgotten thefts gushed out like a geyser of crude oil. The mother shut herself into her fine house for days, aware of the fate awaiting her son. Criminal justice was not the delicate, lenient matter it has become in these enlightened times – not in 1921, and *certainly* not in Italy. Fabrizio was found guilty of burglary and sentenced to be hung.

The whole village crowded the streets on the

morning of Fabrizio's execution. His mother was up by the front, swathed in funeral black, inconsolable. Fabrizio was marched up to the gallows, manacled hand and foot. The executioner read off the crimes for which he was being sentenced.

"Is there any last thing you'd like to say before you die?" he asked Fabrizio, rolling up his paper.

Fabrizio looked up for the first time, eyes searching the crowd. "Yes!" he said, "If you would allow it, sir… before I go, I would love to kiss my mother goodbye."

The executioner looked between the condemned man and his mother. "Very well," he said, "bring her up."

One of the other villagers helped the woman up to the scaffold. Trembling, she embraced her son for the last time in their lives. Fabrizio leaned forward slowly, as though to kiss her. Then he lunged forward with the speed of a snake, his teeth latching onto his mother's nose.

Shrieking, the old woman tried to pull back, but her son's jaws were strong and quick, and he bit down all the harder on her nose, until he had completely ripped it off with his teeth. All the villagers around him were screaming and yelling at Fabrizio in uncomprehending horror. The executioner, himself, tore strips from his shirt to staunch the flow of blood.

"Monster!" he snarled at Fabrizio, "How *dare* you commit such a *blasphemy* on your own mother with your end so close as this?!"

The mother stared out at her son through her tears of pain. Fabrizio, her provider and caretaker of fourteen years, glared at her with a chilling disdain she had never known from him, before turning to spit out her nose.

"I want my mother to look in the mirror every day, and realize that she sent her son, at twenty years old, to his death." He swallowed with difficulty, voice cracking. "Yes, I stole. When it started, I was a little boy. We were poor and desperate… but she accepted everything I brought her without ever asking, 'Son, how did you get this?'"

Spittle flew across his lips to his mother's bloodstained cheeks. "You were not a good mother. All these years… did you know and not care? Or did you not care to know? If you'd really loved me, you could have stopped me, could have pulled me aside and showed me right from wrong. But no… even when we *weren't* destitute, you *liked* it all, loved the free ride too much to risk tipping the boat with such worries."

He bowed his head. The executioner flung the noose around Fabrizio's neck, and he was hung.

Part II

Grandpa Badalament

Father's Father

Meet Louis Badalament

My Grandfather, Louis Badalament, is the man I am proudly named after. He was the youngest son of Anthony and Rose Badalamenti, who had emigrated from Italy. Tony, Grandpa's father, was an accomplished entrepreneur in the banana business, and was a celebrated figure in his community. Tony, for instance, was the first produce dealer in Michigan who thought to use trucks – at a time when horse-drawn carriages were still in widespread use. In time he became one of the biggest banana wholesalers in the county. Even as he saw to his own business, Tony was still generous enough to help other up-and-coming entrepreneurs.

Grandpa Badalament had always aspired to become an engineer, pursuing a degree in engineering at the University of Detroit. But not long after he'd finishing the third of a five-year program, World War II broke out and Grandpa enlisted in the Air Force. He returned home to Michigan to find his father ill. My great-uncle Pete was now running the family business and he needed his brother's help. So, again, Grandpa volunteered his services for the greater good.

Grandpa tried to resume his engineering studies, but the long hours demanded by the produce industry and his studies were too exhausting, and he soon gave up engineering for good to work at Badalament Bananas full-time. In time, he would come to meet an actress, Grace Costello, and win her heart and hand in marriage.

Not long after the birth of his first son – my Uncle Mike – Grandpa Badalament was first lieutenant in the Air Force reserves and was recalled into service in the Korean War. Following the Korean War, Grandma and Grandpa had five other children including my father, Robert. After that, Grandpa continued to work at Badalament Bananas, and in time, he came to preside as head of the company. He only recently retired at age 84! Grandpa Badalament is one of the quiet, unsung heroes – never flashy or ostentatious, but diligent and hard-working, devoted to providing for his family.

Quotes He Lived By

- *"Procrastination is the thief of time."*
- *"Don't say 'snow,' it makes me cold!"*
- *"The pearly dews can kiss the skies, the bees can kiss the butterflies, the pearly dews can kiss the grass… and you, my friend, farewell."*
- *"If you lose your head in business, your shirt will follow."*
- *"Never complain, never explain."*
- *"Be a sponge."*
- *"Son, Thomas Jefferson wrote in the Declaration of Independence that we're entitled to the pursuit of happiness. Not happiness itself, mind you… we've all got to pursue that on our own."*
- *"You have to forgive your wife for the very reason you married her."*
- *"Pioneers end up with arrows in their backs."*
- *"Be a marine!"*
- *"On my feet, I'm an ass, on my ass I'm a genius, so I think I'll sit down."*
- *"I'm too light for heavy work and too heavy for light work."*
- *"You can step on a man's shoes without taking away their shine."*

Chapter Seven

LAWN ENFORCEMENT

Sterotypes are something each of us has to shoulder, yet as pervasive as they are, it's worth remembering that stereotypes don't happen all at once, and they aren't eternal. Italians are an excellent case in point. It wasn't long ago, in American history…

…before we were garlic-scented, tomato-stained, dough-flipping pizza peddlers…

…before we were horse-head-chopping, deal-making Mafioso godfathers…

...before (*Heaven help us*) we were mushroom-chomping, koopa-stomping, mustache-sporting, princess-saving plumbers...

...Italians were simply known as dirty lowlifes and ignoramuses—a lesson my great-grandfather learned the hard way.

Tony crossed the Atlantic at the turn of the century, leaving the boot of Italy to settle in the glove of Michigan. Prior to this fateful ocean voyage, my great-grandfather's name had been Antonio *Badalamenti*, but at Ellis Island, the final 'i' was dropped in hopes of making it more pronounceable for his fellow Americans. After working hard for several years, Tony had saved enough money to move down to the western side of Detroit and buy himself a new home in a respectable neighborhood.

However respectable Tony figured his neighbors might be, they weren't thrilled to learn that an *Italian* would be moving in, with his wife and five kids, to live among them. Heated muttering and the shaking of heads prevailed as Tony's new house was constructed, but they were decent enough to leave well enough alone. The neighbors consoled themselves that as far as inferior heritage went, you could still do a lot worse than Italians.

One individual, however, was willing to go a step further. Tall and white-haired in his early thirties, Lieutenant Saw was every bit as hard and steely as the tool that shared his name. He was also a terribly nosy man – everybody's business was his business. While it's impossible to say whether Saw was actually more bigoted than his peers, he alone was willing to act upon his bias. The morning Tony moved into his new home, Lieutenant Saw paid Tony a neighborly visit. Tony was setting down some boxes, when a knock came at his door, and he answered it to find Saw milling about on his front porch. Very few people, even law-abiding citizens, have the self-assurance to not find a uniformed officer at their doorway disquieting.

"Good morning, officer," Tony said, "am I in some kind of trouble?"

"Why? Have you done anything I should know about?" Lieutenant Saw asked.

Tony quickly recollected his activities over the past few days and replied, "No."

"Then I suppose you're not." Saw dusted off some paint flakes that had fallen on his hat. "I understand that you're new here, Mr....?"

"Badalament." Tony offered.

"Baw-doll...?" Saw grimaced, flashing his teeth. "What's that... *French*?!"

"Italian." Tony told him.

Saw dragged out a breath. "Some consolation, at least," he muttered, dully. "As I was saying, you're new here, so I'm advising you to stay out of trouble. You said you're Eye-talian... now, I don't know how they do things in Little Italy, but I won't stand for any monkeyshines around here."

Tony smiled. "I'm sure that won't be a problem, officer."

"Let's hope not," Saw warned, "for your sake."

Tony talked with Lieutenant Saw a while longer, oblivious of the long history of violence behind the policeman's career—the broken bones and busted organs. Often people Saw arrested had to be sent to the hospital before they did time in a cell. After being nasty and insulting throughout their conversation, Saw concluded that Tony was relatively harmless and unworthy of his time, and turned to leave.

"By the way," Saw said, by way of parting, "you'd do well to plant some grass over all *this*," waving a hand towards the undeveloped topsoil surrounding Tony's new home.

What kind of idiot does he take me for?! Tony wondered, resentfully. But instead of voicing this thought, he fixed the police officer with an impish smile. "No… I figured it'd be a better idea to set up a barn out back and leave the land as is – makes it better for raising my cows on."

Suffice it to say that the joke completely went over the policeman's head, particularly the bit about it actually *being* a joke.

Eyes bulging with horror, Saw spun around, and cut a straight path to his station. All that day, Saw relayed the shocking news to all his fellow officers, and when his shift ended later that day, he spread the word to everyone else he knew.

"Did you hear?!" buzzed Saw, "There's an idiot Italian who just moved in, and he told me – straight to my *face* – that he was going to be bringing cows to live with him… actual mooing, cud-chewing *cows*!"

The neighborhood was scandalized.

"That moron can't bring those lumbering animals to our suburbs!" cried the town librarian, "This is Michigan, not *Wisconsin*!"

"What else did you expect from an Italian?"

"Those things will wander straight into oncoming traffic!"

"Cow pies will be *everywhere*!"

It didn't take that long for Lieutenant Saw to work the community into a frenzied uproar. Everyone agreed that they couldn't allow cattle in their town. Saw collected dozens of signatures for the eviction of Tony Badalament, and led a great crowd of concerned citizens up to Tony's house.

What awaited them was a sight for Saw to see.

Tony Badalament's lush bent lawn was trimmed to match the crisp fineness of a professional golf green, with roses, azaleas, begonias, and chrysanthemums set in rows along the walkway. To their further astonishment, a set of small metallic spouts extended out from the grass, shooting out spurts of water in a wide circle.

"A *sprinkler system*!" sighed one of the women. "I can't believe it!"

None of them could… automatic lawn sprinklers were still a top-dollar innovation at this time, and Tony was the only one in miles who had one installed. It was undeniably the best lawn on the block, and not by accident. Tony had gotten wind of the gossiping, and had hired a professional landscaper from a local golf course to make sure there was nothing anyone could complain about.

"So when will the cows come home, Lieutenant Saw?" someone in the crowd chided.

And to this, Saw had nothing to say.

Twenty-five years down the road, Tony was driving along to work one Sunday morning, when he happened to spot a familiar face shuffling down the sidewalk. Saw was retired from the police force, his step slowed from all the years walking his beat. Tony pulled over by the crosswalk coming up.

"Hey, Saw, where're you headed?"

"Church," said Saw.

It was half-a-mile to church. Tony had been acquainted with Saw long enough to know that the man had never owned his own car.

"Need a lift?" asked Tony.

"You sure?"

"Sure I'm sure."

Saw got in. He was very quiet at first, not even

watching the road. He only spoke when Tony had pulled into the church parking lot.

"I've got to hand it to you," he said, "All this time, you've always been such a good neighbor, and all this time, I caused you a lot of heartache."

"Forget about it," said Tony.

"No, I…"

"Forget it. It's in the past."

Saw grinned and let himself out of the car, waving at Tony as he pulled away.

Chapter Eight

X-Ray Scanner

Tony Badalament's wife, Rose, fell ill one day – complaining of pains in her chest – but no one could find what precisely was ailing her. So Tony made arrangements to have her examined at the Mayo Clinic – a world-famous hospital in Rochester, Minnesota, packed with the brightest doctors and the best that medical care had to offer. After a thorough evaluation, including X-rays, Rose's physician returned with her results. His face had stiffened into a grave expression as he led Rose and Tony into a consultation room, and asked them to sit down.

"I've got some bad news for you." the doctor told them, pointing to a set of radiographs he had hung on a view box. "As you can see, Rose has an enormously enlarged heart."

Rose went totally still in her chair. She absorbed the bad news with a dry throat and watery eyes, squeezing her husband's hand for comfort.

"I'm surprised Rose could even walk into this office," the doctor continued solemnly. "She has a severe case of congestive heart failure and we don't have a lot of options."

Tony's gaze was pinned to the X-rays--staring as though hypnotized. "I'm no doctor," Tony said, "I never made it past the third grade, but are you sure..."

"Yes," the doctor interrupted, "I'm sure."

"...are you sure those are my *wife's* X-rays? I may not be a doctor, but I'm an expert when it comes to my Rosie, and she's just not *that* big, doc!" Tony insisted, pointing to the X-rays.

The doctor looked between the films and the woman in the chair with an expanding gape of amazement. Now that he'd brought it up, the thickness of the ribcage and pelvis were bizarrely disproportionate for a woman of Rose's slim stature. He hurriedly excused himself, taking the X-rays out to be reanalyzed. Some time later, he returned with the correct films and a significantly less dire diagnosis.

Chapter Nine

Will Al Play?

In 1939, my Grandfather was a high school senior at University of Detroit High School. U of D High was – and is – an all-boys college preparatory school run by the Jesuits, renowned not only for its academic prowess, but also for being a perennial football powerhouse. Despite a relatively small enrollment, U of D's football program was so outstanding that its team – the Cubs – qualified to play in the larger City of Detroit Metropolitan League, rather than the more modest Catholic League. The final game of the 1939 season matched the U of D High Cubs against their eternal rival, the Cooley High Cardinals. The two teams were tied for first place, meaning that the winning school would be the City of Detroit Champion.

Now, the football of my grandfather's time was not quite the same game that's played today. Leather helmets without facemasks and inferior padding afforded the players little protection. Early in the second half, U of D's All-City and All-State star fullback, Al Schmidt, was sidelined with a leg injury. The fallen hero was carried off the playing field, and the game ended in a 12 to 12 tie – prompting a playoff game for the league championship.

The rematch was scheduled for the following Saturday. Al was back attending classes that Monday, limping feebly on crutches. All of Grandpa's classmates were uneasy. Football was a second religion at U of D High and the thought of locking horns with the powerful Cooley High Cardinals without Al Schmidt made the student body shudder. But what could anybody do?

In desperation, a small band of Al Schmidt's teammates took it upon themselves to visit Saint Bonaventure's Capuchin Monastery in downtown Detroit to visit a very special person, Father Solanus Casey. He was an unassuming Capuchin monk renowned for working miracles. He gave new distinction to the word 'holy.'

People whispered that Father Solanus could read minds, give prophetic advice, and cure diseases through prayer. In short, Father Solanus was a true phenomenon – the closest thing to a living, breathing saint. And to have someone like that within driving distance is a very fine thing, indeed.

So the small group of football players entered St. Bonventure's Friary and quickly found Father Solanus. He was an unpretentious but distinguished monk, balding with a long grey beard, horn-rimmed glasses and a brown robe. Humbly, and with great emotion, the boys explained their plight and Father Solanus listened to them with gentle patience. Once they were done they asked, "Will Al play?" A long spell of quiet followed their harrowing question. Fr. Solanus thought and prayed with the boys. And then the answer came to light, "Boys, don't worry. Al will play!"

The jubilant football players thanked Fr. Solanus profusely, leaving St. Bonaventure's with spirits soaring. Fr. Solanus' prediction spread throughout the halls of U of D High from boy to boy and from scholastic to priest, until practically the whole school went home convinced that Al would be suited up for the big game. Day after day, U of D held out its hopes that this morning, Al Schmidt would arrive at school with his leg healed, all set to scrimmage with his team for the big game on Saturday. And day after day, his schoolmates winced to hear the creak of those crutches, to see poor Al hobbling along limply from class to class – no perceptible sign of improvement at all. Pessimism sank over the school like a sickening stench.

Much as the Cubs would have liked to postpone it, the day of the big rematch against Cooley High arrived. To his school's astonishment, Al Schmidt was witnessed suiting up with the rest of the Cubs, but emerging from the locker room with a noticeable limp. When the game started, Al was not in the starting lineup; his position was filled by a teammate, Gerry Leone. The game was truly a classic gridiron battle, both teams giving it their very best. Cooley High got a first down within U of D's 5-yard line, but miraculously, U of D held Cooley from scoring and took the ball over at their own 2-yard line.

They battled bitterly down to the 32-yard line. It was 4th down in a scoreless tie during the closing minutes of the game. U of D called timeout and Al Schmidt staggered onto the field for his first and only play of the game. Al was not only the team's All-State fullback, he was also their place-kicker. Victory rode on his completing a 39-yard field goal. The ball was snapped and Al kicked it right down the center of the uprights. When time had expired, U of D had defeated Cooley High 3-0; the undisputed 1939 City of Detroit Metropolitan League High School Football Champions. Silence reigned in the U of D stands, all awed at having witnessed another of Father Solanus' miracles. Not another second passed, however, before the spectators erupted in a torrent of wild cheers and applause.

• • •

Afterword: *Fr. Solanus Casey passed away in July of 1957. His body is buried inside the church of Saint Bonaventure's Friary in Detroit, Michigan. He receives thousands of visitors annually. In 1995, he was elevated to Venerable Solanus Casey of the Roman Catholic Church and is – at the time of this writing – two steps away from sainthood.*

Chapter Ten

Banana Landmine

Although Grandpa Badalament enjoyed his work, he never imagined the banana wholesale business would garner any sort of widespread interest. So when a phone call came, asking whether or not he had the time for a live radio interview about his job, he was quite taken aback.

After he said "yes," they told him they'd hang up and call back in the next five minutes. Excitedly, Grandpa called his family members over, and they all gathered around their radio, tuning the dial to the proper frequency. They all shushed each other pointedly when the phone rang and Grandpa picked it up.

"Hey, hey, hey!" an energetic young man shouted over a chord of theme music. "You're listening to W-I-U-E radio with your host, Dave-in-the-morning!"

"It's nice in the morning with Dave-in-the-morning!" sang his pre-recorded chorus.

"We're speaking live with Mr. Louis Boddle-omunt. Did I say that right?"

"Almost." Grandpa said, smiling patiently.

"Cool! Can I call you 'Lou?'" Dave-in-the-morning asked.

"If you want." Grandpa agreed. It was a little disconcerting, having his own voice bouncing back at him a second later from his own radio. He wished his sons would shut it off, or at least take it out of his office.

"So, Lou, I understand you run a banana warehouse, is that right?"

"That's right," Grandpa said, "I'm one of the owners at Badalament Bananas."

"Where do you grow all these bananas of yours?"

Grandpa laughed. "Actually, sir… our company is *called* Badalament Bananas, but they're not actually *our* bananas. We don't grow them ourselves."

"Well whose are they?" Dave-in-the-morning asked keenly.

"All the big-name banana distributors like Chiquita, Del Monte, and Dole ship some of their bananas to us," He paused, trying to think what else he could add. "A lot of our distributors grow their bananas in several Central American countries: Colombia, Ecuador, Honduras, Panama, Guatemala and Costa Rica. When we get them, we store them and cure them…"

"Cure?" said Dave-in-the-morning, seizing avidly upon the pun. "Why, what's ailing 'em? Yellow spotted fever?"

"It's just a term we use." Grandpa explained, over Dave's laugh track. "In the business, 'curing' is a process of ripening the bananas in the various stages of ripeness which our customers demand."

"That's great!" the radio host said, "but then what do you do?"

"Well then, we sell the bananas to different fruit

markets around the Michigan area."

"Question: When they come in, how yellow are they?"

The radio microphones caught the sound of background chuckling.

"Not yellow at all, sir... they're quite green when they arrive, otherwise they'd ripen too fast. Besides, some customers *like* to buy their bananas a little on the green side, others want them with more color."

"Sure, it's a free country!" Dave-in-the-morning quipped, his voice pumped with high-octane enthusiasm. "So, the question I know's on all our minds is... which bananas are the best?"

"I beg your pardon?" Grandpa asked, a little uneasy now.

"Of all the different bananas companies, whose are the best... the biggest... the longest-lasting and most scrum-diddly-umptious?" He laughed buoyantly. "You'd know better than anyone else, Lou, you're the one that stocks them!"

Everyone gathered in Grandpa's office fell silent. It was an innocent question, but Dave-in-the-morning couldn't have picked a more dangerous thing to ask a man in Grandpa Badalament's position.

Supposing he were to announce on public radio that Chiquita bananas were simply the best, what then? Word would get back to the people at Del Monte and Dole, who would take their business to other, more appreciative warehouses.

After a second, Grandpa cleared his throat. "The best bananas are the ones the retailers make the most money with."

Dave-in-the-morning chortled and clapped into his microphone. "You are *the man*, Lou!"

"I try to be." Grandpa said.

"Well, we're going to take a break now, but stay tuned! When we return – an insider's account into the dark world of pharmaceuticals – when *will* these people learn?" As the theme music faded into a toothpaste commercial, the phone line went dead and everyone, including Grandpa, breathed a grateful sigh of relief.

Chapter Eleven

Another Satisfied Customer

Grandpa Badalament's business catered to all sorts of markets. Bananas were brought in to be processed and cured, then shipped out to be sold and consumed. People from the small Mom-and-Pop shops might drive over in a pickup and buy a few boxes, while the big chain supermarkets might send an 18-wheeler and have it packed chock-full.

As a businessman, Grandpa was both diligent and talented enough to win the respect of all the local produce vendors, and most of his customers were pleasant enough people to service. As with everything, however, life would sometimes throw a curveball. One customer from a smaller market drove up to the warehouse one morning in a brown station wagon.

Business transactions at Badalament Bananas took place at a station that resembled the desk of an inner-city bank teller. Between cashier and customer stood a thick wall of bulletproof glass, with a hole just big enough for passing money through. Grandpa Badalament was manning the register when the small shopkeeper bustled up.

"Give me twenty boxes of your best bananas." he ordered.

"Sure thing," Grandpa agreed. My father – still in high school at the time – was sweeping the floor not far from where they stood.

"Bob," Grandpa called to my father, "put twenty boxes in this gentleman's car."

Loading the man's car was nothing to Bob. He'd filled and emptied hundreds of trucks since his start in the family business. Under the shopkeeper's shifty watch, the brown station wagon was packed with twenty boxes in just a few, short minutes.

They returned inside, and Bob let himself in on Grandpa's side of the glass. When Grandpa rang up the customer's bill, the man glared at it, lip curled. "What is *this*?" he demanded, stabbing the total with an indignant finger. "Your son only put nineteen cases in my car, not twenty!"

"No, I...!" Bob began.

He would have gone on defending himself, but Lou Badalament kicked Bob swiftly in the shin underneath the counter. Angry as he was, Bob was smart enough to let his father do the talking.

"I'm terribly sorry, sir." Grandpa soothed. "Would you like my son to run that last box into your car?"

"Can't!" the customer said, quickly. "My schedule's too tight, and I've wasted enough time here already!"

Grandpa sighed. "All right then, we'll only charge you for nineteen boxes." He swiftly keyed up a new bill and pushed it through the slot for the shopkeeper to look over. Smiling, the man counted out his cash, passed it over, and left.

"Dad, I know I put twenty boxes in his car!" Bob spoke at last.

"I know you did, Bob." Grandpa assured his son. He handed the receipt to my father. "I charged him an extra twenty-five cents per box – made up for the one he stole from us. This way, I don't lose a customer, he gets to drive away pleased with himself, and I still get paid what I'm owed." He shrugged his shoulders easily. "Everyone wins."

Chapter Twelve

Highs and Lows

Mike was the oldest of the six Badalament children. On weekends, he and his brothers would accompany their father to his warehouse and do whatever needed doing at Badalament Bananas: filling and stacking boxes, shoveling snow in winter, and loading and unloading the trucks. At times, however, Mike would swear – wretchedly – that that was *all* they were good for in their father's opinion. This thought was especially gut-scraping whenever the Hi-Lo—his father's forklift—rolled by.

It wasn't a racecar, it wasn't a fighter jet, but Mike had wanted to climb behind its wheel since the first day he'd laid eyes on it - despite the fact that his father had expressly forbidden it, many times. He was all of thirteen now, a *bona fide* teenager. If he couldn't legally drive a car, at least he could drive that. The Hi-Lo couldn't even exceed ten miles an hour.

Maybe he was young, but compared to others his age, he was extremely responsible and competent—not to mention better educated. Yet every time Mike would drop into the seat of the forklift, his father would stomp out, barking, "Get off that damned Hi-Lo right now, Mike!"

One afternoon, Mike's father had to go to a business lunch, leaving Mike at the warehouse. Mike held back a few minutes, even after his father had driven out of sight. Then he hopped onto the Hi-Lo's scratched-up cushion and popped the ignition key in. Oh, what a thrill—operating that grimy yellow machine! Back and forth he steered it, taking palettes stacked with enough boxes to crush a man flat, and hoisting them high over his head. What did his father know anyway? He'd show them how responsible he was!

None of the other warehouse workers did anything to stop Mike's joyride. They'd seen Mr. Badalament chew Mike out on several occasions, but they didn't want to risk angering the boss' oldest son. It was the dream Mike had always known it would be… until a moment's absent-mindedness sent Mike plowing the forklift's enormous, steely prongs straight through a wall. The other workers whirled around or ran out from other rooms to see where the large, grinding smash had come from. Horrified, Mike shifted gears and eased the Hi-Lo back out, but the deed was done. A gaping hole now hung in the middle of the wall, with a fine pile of drywall dust collected on the bottom.

Mike glanced about. Some of the other workers looked as frozen and dismayed as he, while others were biting back chuckles. Mike switched the Hi-Lo off, jumped from its seat, dashed to his father's office, flung himself in a chair, and cried. He was petrified by the thought of how his father was going to punish him… but there was no real way of covering up what he'd done. Bracing himself for the worst, Mike did the only thing he could do to minimize the damage. He picked up the phone, got in contact with his father, and blubbered out a full confession.

His father told Mike to wait for him in the office. Hours later, the doorknob turned, and he stepped inside.

"Come over here, Mike."

Mike shuffled to his father's side. Whatever his father had in store for him, he knew he deserved it. He would suffer the howling tirade, surrender his privileges, and work day and night until his father was paid back.

"The reason I didn't want you to drive the Hi-Lo," he told Mike gently, "was because I didn't want you or one of the employees to get hurt."

Mike waited, but that was all there was to his father's rant. "I figured you thought I was just a dumb kid… that I wasn't mature enough."

"Well, you're not there *yet*," his father conceded to the sniffling, tear-streaked boy, "but some day soon you will be, Mike. For the time being you must promise to obey me and not go on the Hi-Lo without me present."

"Yes, Dad," Mike promised, "But what about the wall?"

"The wall will be repaired. For now, let's just say you've learned a lesson the hard way. At any rate, I've poked a few holes in these walls, myself," he said, with an empathetic wink.

Chapter Thirteen

Starr Quality

One of Grandpa Badalament's favorite stories involves Steve, his youngest son. Steve could play the drum with both skill and zeal. Whenever he was idle, with his hand flat against a wall or tabletop, his fingers would come alive against the surface – jumping and tapping like a secretary racing the clock to finish a report. As deeply as Steve enjoyed *playing* drums, however, his greatest passion was *building* them.

Steve knew drums from their screws to their

skins, and had versed himself in which materials produced the finest intonations. In time, the exquisite design and craftsmanship of Steve's work came into very high demand. Drum enthusiasts the world over agreed; no finer product existed than those fashioned by Steve. He came to be regarded as a living legend, a virtuoso in his field.

One afternoon, a call came through to Steve on his cell phone.

"Is this Steve Badalament?" the caller asked.

"Speaking," Steve said.

"Hello, Mr. Badalament. I'm calling on behalf of Ringo Starr..."

Something caged within Steve's ribs skipped a beat. "Ringo Starr?!" he whispered.

At this stage of his career, Steve was no stranger to celebrity. He dealt with the famous and the gifted on a daily basis, but Steve was one of the many millions whose hearts had been overtaken by the British Invasion - and as a devout drummer, Ringo Starr occupied a special place in Steve's personal pantheon.

The caller responded to Steve's reverence with a good-natured chuckle. "Yes, *the* Ringo Starr. Ringo's heard good things about your line of drums, and he's looking to buy a drum kit for his son's birthday."

"Sure!" Steve agreed, awed, honored and scarcely believing this turn of luck. "Does Ringo have any specifics in mind?"

"Well, he's interested in your titanium model."

"Titanium? Sure thing!" Steve grabbed a scrap of paper, readying himself to take notes.

"There's one thing I should mention before we go further," the caller cautioned.

"Name it," said Steve, confidently.

"Young Mr. Starr's birthday is in a month's time, and before he commissions anything from you, Ringo would like your word that it'll be finished by then."

Steve fell silent, his gut twisting and churning like a winning lottery ticket in a whirring garbage disposal.

"I'm sorry," Steve said, "tell Ringo, with my deepest apologies, that he'd do better to look for drums somewhere else."

"Wait a minute, you're refusing Ringo Starr?" The caller laughed limply. "People don't say 'No' to Ringo Starr."

"I have to," Steve explained, soberly, "Titanium is an extremely strong, hard metal – it takes time to do it full justice. In order to get a kit out to Ringo in just a month, I'd have no choice but to cut corners, and I could never shortchange Ringo Starr. He deserves no less than first-rate workmanship, and if I can't give Ringo my absolute best, then I won't be giving him anything at all."

"Are you serious?" the caller asked, flabbergasted.

"Yes – that's my final answer."

Steve hung up on the man, sighing deeply. His cell phone rang a few moments later, and he flipped it open. He frowned - it was the exact same caller he'd talked to.

"Listen, Steve… about that last call of ours…"

"Yeah?"

"Ringo was listening in on the line when we talked the first time. He's with me right now, in fact."

There was a muffled exchange, and suddenly Steve's ear was filled with a voice he had heard countless times on the radio and records; low, older, but with a singularly distinguishing Liverpool accent.

"Hullo, Steve. I was really touched by all those things you said, and I'd still love to buy a set of your drums. Take as much time as you need to get it right."

"So, a belated birthday present, then?"

Ringo laughed. "Something like that."

Part III

Grandma Vitale

Mother's Mother

MEET FRANCES LEONE VITALE

Frances Leone was born in Detroit, Michigan as the third of four children. Her father was a produce wholesaler, and her mother was a stay-at-home mom with a passion for crochet. She enjoyed a comfortable, easy childhood with enough time for play, work and school. However, at age sixteen, she had to shoulder more adult responsibilities for herself, after her father suffered a fatal heart attack.

As a young woman, Grandma worked as a typist for an insurance company. She first met Procopio Vitale in 1951, when she was playing baseball at a picnic. They were married sometime later that same year. She quit her job at the insurance firm and devoted her time and energy to helping Grandpa Vitale in a variety of business ventures; Vitale Fish Market in 1952, then Sammy's Fruit Market in 1954 and Whittier Nursery in 1959. Even-

tually, they found their niche in the produce business, with a little store called Pete and Frank's Fruit Ranch in Eastpointe, Michigan.

Grandma Vitale exemplified the phrase, "the wind beneath my wings." She quietly worked alongside Grandpa, performing a broad scope of duties with skill and vigor—everything from bookkeeping and cashiering to arranging flowers and fashioning bows to tie around them. In time, she became the proud mother of six children and groomed them to become responsible and productive people, encouraging each to do what they could so that they could be depended upon to contribute to the family. Her fifth child, Providence, is my mother. I'm not the only one who has noticed that she inherited many of Grandma Vitale's finer qualities.

Quotes She Lived By

- *"A little bit more and you can go first class."*
- *"Put a nickel in it!"*
- *"The head that doesn't talk is called a squash."*
- *"I have champagne taste on a beer pocketbook."*
- *"The day's melting away like ice cream."*
- *"I'm going to call your father!"*
- *"Make every trip a good trip."*
- *"Don't put off for tomorrow what you can do today."*
- *"Show them where you live!"*
- "Figlio *Mia!"*
- *"This will cover a multitude of sins."*

Chapter Fourteen

Cast Offs

When Grandma and Grandpa Vitale retired from the produce business, they bought a second home near San Diego, California. My family would fly from our Michigan home and visit them on summer vacations. When I was twelve, we decided to cross that infamous southern border and visit Mexico. One of the places we explored was a small outdoor marketplace where vendors grilled enchiladas and peddled trinkets from their tents and kiosks.

My oldest cousin, Peter, had bought many souvenirs already, but he wanted to buy one more as a consolation gift for his brother, Philip, who couldn't make the trip, so he entered a shaded shop to search for something appropriate. The saleslady said nothing as Peter looked around, finally selecting a black T-shirt featuring Bart Simpson slinging out the Spanish equivalent of "Don't have a cow, man!" The saleswoman smiled thinly as Peter paid for it, slipping the cash into a little cigar box.

Peter turned out of the shop. The door had just shut behind him when he noticed something wrong about his new purchase; the seams under the sleeves appeared to have been sewn by a distracted five-year-old.

"Grandma!" he called out. The whole family was shopping in very close proximity to one another, so when Peter beckoned his grandmother over, she came with my mother, Providence, who'd been shopping right alongside her. He showed her the shirt.

Striding inside, Grandma flattened the ragged shirt on the saleslady's counter. "My grandson bought this for his brother," she explained, "but it's got a big rip in it."

The saleslady eyed the un-sewn seam as though it

were a boring portrait in a dull museum.

"We'd like to return this shirt and get our money back," Grandma said.

"No," the saleslady said in stilted English, "No money. You buy, you keep."

"But this is damaged." Grandma argued, "We want a good shirt, or we want our money back."

The woman's lips creased into the delighted smirk of a spoiled child. "No, lady. No money." She repeated. But she pointed to the shirts as though to say, 'you can pick another shirt.' Then she turned around, pretending to be busy.

"Well then," Grandma sighed serenely, her eyes narrowing. "I suppose there's nothing we can do but pick out a new one."

The saleslady grinned indifferently.

Grandma Vitale dropped the damaged T-shirt on the floor. Peter bent to pick it up, but the tiniest shake of his grandmother's head stopped him. He watched as Grandma moved to a display of T-shirts.

"What do think of this one?" she questioned, shaking it out of its fold.

"It's nothing special." Peter decided.

"I agree," Grandma replied, letting it float to the floor. "What about this one?" she asked, unfolding another.

"Junk," Providence said, smiling.

Grandma nodded, turning it inside-out and slinging it over her shoulder.

The shop had at least two hundred shirts on display, each folded as neatly as an envelope. My Grandma took shirt after shirt – pinching them at the shoulders and flipping them around to examine their backs before tossing them aside. Soon enough, Providence and Peter were joining in on her act, crumpling up shirts like empty hamburger wrappers without the slightest glance in the saleslady's direction. It wasn't until about sixty of her shirts had been pitched about that the saleslady started becoming alarmed.

Another American tourist strode into the shop, stopping cold as he stared about. The once-tidy shop was quickly taking on the look of a grungy college dorm room.

"Still haven't found anything worth buying." my Grandma told the man blithely, as he spun on his heel and left.

"¡*Un momento!*" the saleslady finally cried. "¡*Un momento, por favor, señora!*" She dashed into a backroom, returning with a fresh Bart Simpson T-shirt. The three of them inspected the shirt as they had all the others, and found it to be stitched perfectly.

"Thank you so much!" Grandma said sweetly.

Chapter Fifteen

Riding Roughshod

He pulled into Murray's Auto World in the most rusted, busted, dilapidated pickup truck the salesmen had ever seen this side of a landfill. In place of glass, one side had a garbage bag duct-taped to its window frame. Dents dimpled the truck's frame like acne scars, while a collection of silver scratches marked up the sides like old battle wounds. Most of the paint had worn away—random patches of turquoise clung bitterly between the rust and the dust—while clear ridges of glue held the rearview mirrors in place. By the looks of things, someone had lobbed an M-80 onto the hood years ago, leaving most of it blackened.

The driver hopped from the cab of the truck and walked briskly into the service center. He was clearly a farmer – his appearance and stench suggesting he'd just driven in from a solid day's work. He was bow-legged and sweat-stained, with a forest of chest hairs sprouting from the neck of his soiled shirt. His overalls showcased the sort of grass, dirt, blood and beer stains worthy of Rorschach's inkblot tests.

All Murray's salesmen suddenly found other things to do. Two of the salesmen hastened into the men's room simultaneously while a third stepped over to a browsing woman and began an unwanted sales pitch.

Murray, the owner of the dealership, sighed. "Sir." he said, stepping forward seriously, "Excuse me, sir?"

"Hello!" the farmer slurred—his breath a wilting fusion of chewing tobacco, stale beer and digestive medicine, strong enough to prompt the owner to step back. "I wanna buy a car!"

"That's great, sir. Why don't we step outside?

We've got an excellent selection of used cars out there."

The farmer's gaping smile faltered slightly. "I'm not interested in any used clunker."

"What were you looking for?"

"A Cadillac!" he crowed. "Always wanted a Caddy, and tonight I'm gonna motor home in one!"

The other salesmen all jerked a hard look at the farmer, even the one who was handling another customer. Murray had to suppress an impulse to laugh in the farmer's face.

"Mr. Murray, sir?" called a younger man, stepping forward, "If you don't mind, I'd be glad to do the honors!"

Murray waved this fellow over to his side, gratefully. "I'd like you to meet Jason Zubrick. He'll be taking over for me from here."

Fresh out of college, Zubrick was the youngest and latest addition to Murray's sales crew. He looked the farmer over, and held out his hand.

"Welcome to Murray's!"

"Bo Swottsworth." the farmer introduced, pumping his arm.

"You're interested in a Cadillac? We've got a couple of good ones over here, including the Eldorado Seville—just introduced by GM this year."

"Al-door-raw-dough! What a great name!" Bo hooted.

Zubrick led the farmer through the models inside the spotless showroom, explaining everything he knew about the cars. He opened all the doors of every Cadillac to show Bo their luxurious interiors, popped opened the trunks and let his enthusiastic customer kick each tire. The other salesmen sighed in disbelief when they saw them, letting out soft chuckles and shaking their heads. Starry-eyed daydreamers like Bo Swottsworth had floated in here before. It usually only took one good, hard look at the Cadillacs' price tags to bring them back down to Earth.

A little later, Zubrick returned to the service center alone.

"Where'd your new friend go?" Murray asked, sarcastically.

"He's at the side exit, waiting for us to prep his Cadillacs."

All the salesmen stopped and stared, still-faced.

"Cadillacs?" Murray repeated, "As in more than one?"

"Turns out Mr. Swottsworth is loaded." Zubrick explained, smiling. "He purchased a green Eldorado Seville for himself, a pink Coupe de Ville for his 'Missus,' and a white convertible for his boy."

Mr. Murray's expression scrunched up; Zubrick heard his boss muttering a few choice words beneath his breath.

"Son, there's a lot you've got to learn about people," Murray said, steering him into his office and shutting the door. "Do you honestly think a grungy plow jockey like that has the credit to afford *three* Cadillacs? Because if you're really that gullible, I don't think you're suited to work at this dealership."

But Jason Zubrick gazed evenly. "If I could really sell him Cadillacs, I'd have to be one heck of a fine salesman, wouldn't I?"

"You would be," Murray responded.

"Good enough to deserve a raise?" Zubrick pressed.

"Definitely," his boss said, confidently.

"And your word is your bond."

"Always is."

Jason Zubrick chanced a look back; the other salesmen were gathered around Murray's office door, watching with bemusement. He then reached down into his pocket and pulled out a large wad of crisp new hundred-dollar bills for Murray to count.

"Good old Bo paid in cash. Thanks for the raise, Boss."

Chapter Sixteen

Coffee Fix

Ubaldo always knew where to find his friend, Benito. Old Benito was forever stationed behind the counter of his dark little coffeehouse. How Benito kept in business was a mystery, for no matter how often Ubaldo stopped by his friend's shop, there never was a customer to be seen. Still, Benito was faring better than Ubaldo, who could barely keep his head above water scrambling from debt to debt.

One frosty evening midway through January, Ub-

Coffee Fix

aldo stumbled into the warm coffeehouse. Benito—a sleepy-eyed fellow—observed his friend shaking the snow off the shoulders of a heavily patched sweater.

"What can I pour you?" Benito asked, but the other man shook his head.

"Benito," Ubaldo began, "I'm in a really bad jam. Times are hard, and my rent is up. There's nobody else I can turn to. If you had five hundred dollars you could lend..."

"Of course," Benito answered, tranquilly. He drew what Ubaldo needed from his cash register and handed it over. "I've known hard times, myself. Pay me back at your own convenience."

"I won't forget this!" Ubaldo vowed, "I promise I'll repay you!"

The café's doorbell jingled as he hurried out to his car.

Some time later, in the early days of February, Ubaldo reappeared in high spirits and a newly bought jacket.

"Here it is!" Ubaldo declared, counting the money out on the countertop. "The five hundred dollars I borrowed in January, paid back in full!"

"Ah, that's great." Benito said, spooning sugar into his espresso. "Do me a favor, would you, Ubaldo? Go put it in that jar over there."

Benito pointed to a wide biscotti jar at the end of his counter. It was a funny request, but Ubaldo uncorked the jar, stuffed in the cash and left Benito's shop content.

Benito didn't see Ubaldo again until the first week of March. Once again his friend shuffled into the dim little café—threadbare and casting backwards glances as though creditors were hounding him.

"Things are worse than ever before, Benito. Imposing on your generosity again tears at my heart, but if there's any chance you can lend me even five hundred dollars..."

"Five hundred dollars?" asked Benito. "Not to worry, just take it from the jar."

Ubaldo shot Benito a startled look, but Benito simply went back to vacuuming the floor. He went to the biscotti jar and opened the lid to find the exact same five hundred dollars he'd repaid Benito with—to the bill.

"You're a saint, Benito! I'll bring this right back –

you watch!" Ubaldo promised, rushing out to pay his dues.

April came, and with it, Ubaldo. There was no mistaking which way his luck had gone. His features were gaunt and drawn and his shoulders sagged with the weight of sleepless nights – yet still he was jumpy, rubbing his palms and arms as though he'd spent all night in the cold.

"Benito," Ubaldo said, "I need money again. *Please*. I'm in terrible shape." He wouldn't elaborate further than that.

"Go over to our little jar, the money should be there." Benito said.

Ubaldo approached the biscotti jar, opened it, and reached inside.

"There's no money in here." Ubaldo moaned, poking every square inch of the empty jar with desperate fingertips.

"Hmmm…" Benito hummed, "Did you pay me back last time?"

"No. No, I didn't." Ubaldo confessed.

"Ah," Benito said, sadly. "Maybe if you'd returned

what you borrowed, you could've used it now. I'm sorry, my friend, but your cookie jar's empty."

Chapter Seventeen

Elbow Room

Frances boarded a crowded bus one afternoon, and was lucky enough to spot an open seat to take, right away. She was a young woman at this point in time, relieved to be heading home after another day pounding away at her typewriter for her bosses at Michigan Mutual Insurance Company. Dodging around the disembarking passengers, she whizzed right into a seat near the end of the bus, beside some other lady.

The seats along the front of the bus were like those in a car – facing the windshield. The seat she was in, by the bus' rear, was essentially a bench whose back was propped up against a windowed wall, facing a matching bench on the opposite wall. From this terminal at downtown Detroit, this bus cut a nonstop run to the far east side, where Frances lived.

As the bus driver shut the door and the motor rumbled to life, Frances relaxed into the vinyl cushion, content to let the bus and everything within it fade from focus… and then a firm prodding against her shoulder jolted her out of her reverie. An enormous woman was standing beside her.

"*Hi,*" the woman wheezed.

"Hello." Frances replied politely. The woman sharing Frances' bench also looked up.

It was obvious the woman had more to say once she'd caught her breath. She was an august, tubby sort, whose body hung in folds and ripples that reminded Frances of thawing caramel. Granted, a little exhaustion was understandable if she'd had to rush to make the bus – which she had. But this bleary-eyed woman looked almost completely wiped-out, barely able to keep herself upright.

"Awfully sorry for asking this," she spoke again, rubbing roughly at her eyelids, "but you wouldn't object if I just sat on the edge of the seat, next to you?"

The two seated women cast apprehensive looks at each other. Their bench was wide enough for two-and-a-half average people to sit. In other words; three skinny beanpoles could sit together here in perfect comfort. One beanpole and two medium-sized travelers could tolerate the ride.

Frances had a slender frame. The lady beside her was of moderate proportions.

Both of them cringed as the broad hulk over them gave a startling sway forward, only just catching herself from falling on top of them.

"I suppose it's okay with me, if it's okay with you, Miss?" the moderate-sized woman asked Frances.

"Sure, I guess," she said at last.

"*Thanks*," the heavy passenger huffed. The other two ladies huddled over as the fat woman packed herself in, with half her bottom flat against the bench.

Frances, herself, sat scrunched in the middle. She tried letting her thoughts wander aimlessly again, saying nothing when she felt the fat woman slant a small portion of her arm against her own. Minutes passed, and she couldn't help noticing that the weight resting against her felt heavier than earlier. There was also the sound of snoring.

"Is she sleeping?" asked the average-sized passenger, bending over for a better look at the fat woman's half-open mouth.

The fat woman's head had drooped onto Frances' shoulder; she could feel her ear pressing through the fabric of her shirt.

Frances was too well-mannered to wake the larger woman, so she forced a polite little laugh. "Probably should've seen it coming," she said, shifting over an inch or so closer towards the slimmer woman, who, in turn, shifted an inch of herself off the bench.

And, in turn, the fat lady nudged more of herself into Frances, thrusting forward with her feet.

A quarter of an hour later, the situation had turned ridiculous. The great hibernating she-bear had taken over half the bench for herself, and was still flattening Frances into the other woman like a pillow into the headboard. No amount of poking or whispering from either of them could stir this slumbering mountain.

"Oh, *enough of this*!" cried the average-sized woman, grabbing her purse. With difficulty, Frances disentangled herself and tumbled into the aisle, letting the wide giantess fall flat across the rest of the bench. She and the other unfortunate woman got up, grabbing hold of the railing overhead, scowling back at the slumbering woman.

Though her eyes stayed closed, they distinctly saw her smile thickly in their direction as she centered herself upon her bench, snuggling cozily into the vinyl.

Chapter Eighteen

1/2 Off of 1/2 Off

A husband and his wife really loved each other, and in time, this love bore them the fruit of six beautiful children – three boys and three girls, in that order.

Now, it is no easy feat for any parents to see to the needs of so many sons and daughters, and at this early stage in his career, the father was scarcely rolling in cash. Still, the father and his wife were conscientious and resourceful, and were able to devise all sorts of strategies to make ends meet.

In particular, the mother had been able to establish a very shrewd method of buying all her fast-growing kids clothes without breaking the bank. Around the early 1970s, there was a small clothing store known as Barnaby's. Twice every year, at the end of summer and winter, Barnaby's would host an all-day clearance sale known as the "½ Off of ½ Off" sale. As the name suggested, prices for all of Barnaby's regular merchandise was cut to a *quarter* of its standard value – so that an eight-dollar pair of shoes cost only two bucks.

As the mother told her daughter, "You can't *make* them that cheap!"

A lot of careful preparation and planning went into the Barnaby's markdown. The ½ Off of ½ Off sale was the main time for the children to replenish their wardrobe… and the wife knew there'd be competition, sharp and quick as piranhas upon a fallen calf. She would drive over to Barnaby's the night before the momentous discount to case the joint, noting where all the good clothes were being placed by the staff.

At 3 AM that next morning, twelve figures would congregate before the Barnaby's entrance. There was the mother and her six children – but also, the mother's sister, and her children. Huddled together against the chill of morning, they stood waiting for the shop to open its doors, shopping carts at the ready. It actually wasn't that long before other families of cost-conscious customers collected behind them, disgruntled to see others ahead of them.

The line accumulated wider after dawn broke. Still the throng waited the next several hours on... until a Barnaby's clerk finally came over and unlocked the door. As one, the family shot forward, frontrunners in the marathon, dividing every which way. Each individual family member would dash upon a rotating rack of clothes, before anyone else. Seizing the *entire rack* in one wide bear hug, he or she would then dump everything into his or her cart.

The intent behind this tactic was *not* to rob the other Barnaby's shoppers of their chance to buy clothes – the family just wanted to leaf through the selection first, before everyone else took all the good stuff away. Once each family member had filled his or her cart, they would immediately sit down and begin returning the extra merchandise back on the racks, until each child had picked out just what they needed. As their mother had instructed, the children took pains choosing clothes that were a size or so bigger than their actual height – kids grew up so fast, after all.

Barnaby's was a spacious store, and all the family was speedy about sifting through the jeans, shirts, shorts, skirts, blouses and coats, uncovering what they wanted, and hanging what remained back upon its rack. But the other patrons weren't blind to what was happening, here. Twelve individuals – with striking resemblances to one another – were all yanking armfuls of cotton and denim off the best-stocked racks, at the same time?

One after another, the children hustled back around their mother, the clothes they'd gathered lying neatly in their carts. It wouldn't be long before they could take their place at the checkout aisle. Only a few of them were still picking through the racks... including the mother, herself. This was when a perfect stranger came up, bent over the mother's cart, and began rifling through the clothes inside, right alongside the mother.

The family had been shopping at Barnaby's for many years now, but this was unprecedented in the mother's experience… and uncalled for.

"Excuse me, miss," the mother spoke, heatedly, "Don't take clothes out of my cart!"

"Well, you can't possibly take *all* of those," the woman snapped, plucking out something mauve and lacy.

"I'll take what I want!" the mother shot back. "I'll take what I came to get, just like you and everyone else shopping here is gonna take what *they* came for!"

The other woman made to shove her aside. "Well, you don't need two of these coats, and I want one."

The mother slid her shopping cart behind her back side, ready to sit inside it, if she must.

"Look at me, ma'am. I've six kids, and I'm buying for more than one family – my sister has kids of her own. Every cent counts. I'm not going to dither here all day; I only come to Barnaby's *twice* each year for their ½ Off of ½ Off sales. That's the whole rest of the year you've got to yourself! We're all being as quick and quiet as possible."

She took a breath.

"Now, please. It's a big store and there's *tons* of other clothes we haven't touched!"

"I'd like what's in *your* basket!" demanded the woman, reaching around her.

Her hand was shoved away. The woman's eyes widened – along with all the mother's children's – as the mother jerked up a fist.

"Do you want to step outside?" she questioned.

The mother had brought her arm back down quickly.

"The people here at Barnaby's have been very good to us, giving us bargains… so I won't cause a commotion inside their store. But if you're going to raise *this* big a stink, if you're determined to make us go *six months* in clothes we don't really care for… then you leave me no other choice."

There was rage and tiredness in her eyes from having waited outside since early morning with all her children. Aggressiveness was not really part of the mother's character. Even under immense frustration, the worst she usually did was yell. All the same, her challenge was no hollow threat. This busybody had squirmed under her skin; and at a word, she was set to go around to the back of the Barnaby's building and duke it out, one-on-one.

It was a fight the world would never know. The intrusive stranger blanched pale – never having figured on the mother being provoked this far beyond mere squabbling. Meek as could be, she took the mother's advice and whisked away down an aisle of parkas towards the farther end of the store.

"Wow, Mom, where did *that* come from?" asked her daughter.

She and her brothers and sisters were awestruck behind their shopping carts, watching for any new surprises to spring out of their mother. But the strange lady hadn't even slipped from sight, when their mother turned around, the hard glower evaporating.

"Only the best for my children," she stated, hugging her daughter. "Now, if everyone's got what they wanted, then let's head out to the checkout lane. Come on, put a nickel in it."

Chapter Nineteen

Woe Is Me

Edmondo and Salvatore lived as neighbors in a small farming town, years before the advent of radio. This town had served as Edmondo's home for all his life. In thirty years, he had never traveled more than two miles outside it. Salvatore was something of a newcomer, having just moved in from Genoa only a few weeks before.

Nothing delighted the inhabitants of this town quite so much as gossip. Rumor was their wellspring of joy, but their town was somewhat out of the way, and it was a rare pleasure when news of the outside world reached their ears. Most of the time, they could only chat about what was going on in their own community.

It was hard to say what it was about Edmondo that the other townsfolk found so curious and compelling. At first blush one saw a long string of averages. His looks were nice enough, but he wasn't handsome. He was decent, but not virtuous – not poor nor rich, not smart nor dumb, not lazy, but not exactly industrious, either.

Perhaps it was the fact that Edmondo was one of the few people in the town who didn't care for gossip. He wasn't unfriendly, but he preferred to keep his business to himself and didn't pry into the business of others. Paradoxically, whenever something did happen to him, it was all the more interesting to the gossipers when they gathered to talk at the bar.

"Did you hear the latest?" a young tailor asked his fellows one evening, "Edmondo had a fire in his house!"

The rest of them gathered close, pressing for details.

Woe Is Me

"Edmondo's wife, Gianna, told me the story." the tailor reported, "You know how Edmondo likes to smoke his pipe, right? Well, apparently, he wasn't watching where his ashes fell, and they caught on his blanket. Half of the house went up before they could put out the blaze. They bought new clothes from me, but they're also going to have to buy a new bed and build a new wall and roof!"

The others shook their heads.

"Bad thing to happen." said the town preacher.

"Poor Edmondo." sighed the shoemaker.

To the tailor's side, someone snorted loudly. It was Salvatore, sitting the next table over.

"Poor *Edmondo*?" Salvatore scoffed, "He got off lucky! When I was in Genoa, not only did my entire house go up in smoke, the fire also claimed my crops, my barn, and all the animals inside it. All my goats, burned to death!"

"Oh!" cried the fisherman, the others looking on him with a mixture of grievous pity and eagerness. "I'm so sorry to hear it, Salvatore! Tell us what happened."

"It was dreadful…" Salvatore sighed.

For the next week, the talk was all about Salvatore. Wherever he went, passers-by offered their condolences and pumped him for details about his tragedy, which he was always happy to provide. A few considerate souls also thought to see Edmondo, who smiled and said, "We're fine. We're going to make it through."

Two weeks had passed when Edmondo's life took a new and startling turn. An older cousin of Edmondo's stumbled out from a rainstorm into a gaggle of gossipers.

"You're not going to *believe* this," the old woman said, "you know Gianna, my cousin Edmondo's wife? He came home from the market to find that old tart kissing Lucio Conti!"

"*No!*" breathed the preacher.

"Which one's Lucio Conti?" asked the shoemaker.

"The one who paints," the preacher reminded.

"Oh *him*," said the shoemaker, "go on."

"Well, Lucio took off at once, and for all I know, Gianna and Edmondo are still screaming at each other."

"What a bad thing to come home to." the preacher clucked.

"Please…" snapped Salvatore, who had become firmly established as one of the best gossipers in the community, "you act as though no wife has ever kissed another man! You haven't *seen* unfaithfulness the way I have."

Salvatore's lip quivered. "My dear, sweet Claudina," he said, in a hushed voice, "for five years in Genoa, we were husband and wife, until one day I come home to find her with my best friend!" Tears spilled from Salvatore's eyes. "Then she tells me… *laughing*, that she's been seeing other men behind my back since I first proposed to her!"

The town couldn't get enough of Salvatore's old scandal. They picked over the details as Salvatore moaned bitterly over lost love.

Meanwhile, things were not going well for Edmondo. Gianna was still living with him, but there was no warmth between them. What was more startling was that Edmondo's health had taken a turn for the worst. No matter how warmly he dressed, his body was always shaking with chills, and he would hock up phlegm the color of old rust. For the next few weeks, the community watched him struggling back and forth from his house to the hospital, until finally, Gianna announced, miserably, that pneumonia had claimed Edmondo's life. They bore his body to the church, and set him in a coffin. Practically everyone in the town came to pay their last respects.

"It was horrible," said Gianna at the wake, "he didn't go peacefully."

"How did he get it?" asked the preacher.

"He ran out into the storm the night that we fought," Gianna explained, "We thought it was just a cold, at first, but he was having pains in his chest and his body just never cooled down. The worst of it was that he seemed to be losing his mind… talking nonsense until he was babbling the way you do to a baby."

The preacher hung his head. "What a rotten way to go. I'd give up a mountain of gold not to catch anything like his pneumonia."

"*His* pneumonia?!" Salvatore cried. Many people wheeled around to stare at him. "What about *my* pneumonia?! The pains in *my* chest were so agonizing; it was like a family of rats chewing away from the inside. My body was so hot that the blood in my veins boiled like a pot of soup, but I was so cold that I felt as though I had dropped to the bottom of the sea! I was so crazy with the pain; I thought I was a sparrow. Mine was ten times worse!"

In the pause that followed, several dozen sets of eyes either narrowed very coldly, or widened with complete incredulity.

"And I suppose the pneumonia was so bad that it brought you right back to life after it killed you, so you could whine about how very excruciating it was?" asked Gianna.

"Come on then, Salvatore." someone else challenged, "Make us feel sorry for you."

Salvatore's mouth worked itself into all sorts of expressions and shapes, but nothing of consequence came out.

Chapter Twenty

Truth or Consequences

Grandpa Vitale was doing his best not to make a big deal of it, but all his years of hard work and manual labor were beginning to take their toll. Arthritis had slithered through his joints as quietly as rust through old plumbing – already the doctors were giving him medication to ease the aches and pains in his knees. All three of his sons were fully-grown men, but that still left three young daughters to care for. Fran, his youngest, was only two years old. Still, he could see retirement looming ahead in his future, and set out to prepare himself.

Thus, it came to pass in the summer of 1972 that Grandma and Grandpa Vitale decided to treat themselves and their girls to a road trip. They even bought a brand-new car just for the occasion – a 1972 Mercury Marquis station wagon with wood-grained panel siding. Once Lisa, Fran, and Providence were all packed inside, they headed southwest. They crossed through places they'd only seen in geography textbooks — stopping at restaurants, parks, stores, and shows where they could stretch out, have fun, and take pictures.

Of course, there was more behind this outing than simple sightseeing. Grandma and Grandpa were also exploring the real estate, scouting out the best locale for the retirement home they'd build later in life. Michigan was a wonderful state in many respects, but the winters tended to exceed the bitter end, and they'd had their fill of White Christmases.

They had looked at Florida a year earlier, but found it unsuitable. The weather was warm enough, but it was also very muggy and the hurricanes Florida was eternally attracting did nothing to entice them. Humidity was never easy on stiff joints — they needed someplace where precipitation of any kind was a rare occurrence. Friends recommended they try Arizona.

"It's warm, like Florida, but completely bone-dry," they had said. Grandma and Grandpa had agreed, and they set their sights on Tucson.

On they rolled; state after state. They woke up fresh in a motel in Amarillo, Texas, filled their tank, and headed about 285 miles westward down Interstate 40… stopping in Albuquerque, New Mexico for a quick afternoon lunch.

"Al – buh – cur – key," Grandma sounded out to Fran, as they munched burgers at a diner.

"*Alba's Cookie!*" the small two-year-old tried valiantly. After their meal, they shuffled back into their car, Grandpa merging onto I-25, heading south.

"A few more miles, and we'll be out of Albuquerque." Grandma observed, scanning her map.

Grandpa checked the fuel gauge. Its needle hung at an unsettling midway position between a half-full tank and the letter 'E'. He hadn't stopped to refuel at any point since Amarillo, he realized, relieved to spot a gas station coming up, right off the next exit.

Grandpa flicked on his turning light.

"What are you doing?" Grandma Vitale asked, frowning over the top of her map.

"I'm pulling over to get gas." he told her, checking his rearview mirror.

"Not now, honey." she advised, "We'll get gas at the next exit." It just seemed somehow inappropriate to stop for gasoline so soon after they'd eaten!

His face screwed up as though he'd swallowed a bad grape, but he popped the turn signal off and sped past the exit.

It was a couple minutes after one. The sun was shining brilliantly, unobstructed by clouds, trees, or skyscrapers. Ten minutes stretched into thirty as the vast, flat landscape slid by — free of stores, buildings, telephone booths, stoplights, or homes of any sort — just the flat, dry sprawl of the Chihuahuan Desert. The only evidence that other human beings had crossed this wasteland before was the long line of pavement under their tires, and the odd highway sign.

Lisa gawked when she read one of them.

"What the... Gallop: 500 miles? Are they for real?"

"It's probably a town or something, Lisa." Providence guessed.

The sisters chuckled to themselves – what kind of people would name their home 'Gallop?'

"You know what'll eventually happen, right?" said Lisa, snickering. "There'll come a day when some total idiot will see that sign, get out of his car, and actually try and gallop five hundred miles!"

"Maybe it's already happened!" Providence said, pressing up against her window. "Quick, look for skeletons!"

A full hour after bypassing the last exit, the needle on the fuel gauge had slid down a notch.

"I need to go to the bathroom." Lisa moaned.

"Can it wait, sweetie?" Grandma Vitale asked, pleading with her eyes.

"I guess so." Lisa conceded.

Adding to the overall discomfort was the fact that their air conditioner was on the fritz. Grandma tried cranking down the windows, but even with Grandpa driving at maximum speed, the air rushing in was no cooler.

"How much longer 'til we get somewhere, Frances?" Grandpa muttered over the wails of his two-year-old.

Grandma consulted the map again. "It doesn't say," she admitted, "just keep going in this direction, and we should get there." She turned around to her girls. "Why don't you try getting some sleep? We'll wake you up once we're there."

The temperature outside had climbed to the pitch of a good fever, and the idea of sleeping under such oppressive heat was laughable. The girls sat sullenly as their gasoline dwindled even lower.

"We're out of drinks." Providence informed the others some minutes later, shaking an empty thermos upside-down.

"We'll buy more drinks at the next town." Grandma assured.

As the next hour ticked along, they all watched the fuel gauge with the intensity of scuba drivers low on oxygen, until the needle settled right against the red Empty line.

And still they drove. It was like waiting for a guillotine blade to drop – almost mockingly, the station wagon was still running just as fast on fumes as it'd gone on half a tank.

"What do we do when the gas runs out?" Lisa asked. She could see plenty more desert ahead of them – what if they really *did* have to sleep here?

"We'll cross that bridge when we get to it." Grandma answered.

"Looks like we're at that bridge!" Providence mumbled. The car was now slowing down.

"It's just me," Grandpa explained, decelerating smoothly until he could pull over and park by the side of the road.

"Dad, what are we doing?"

"We're not driving any farther." he said, "We don't know how far the next town is, and if we keep driving with no gas, we'll ruin the engine." He thumped the steering wheel. "You girls stay in the car."

He got out from the station wagon, pacing slowly back and forth along the dusty asphalt. When he caught sight of another car riding down the freeway, Grandpa shouted out, flailing his arms until the driver of the car pulled alongside.

"Looks like you're in a spot of trouble." their Good Samaritan observed, looking through the window at the three sweltering little girls.

"We're out of gas," Grandpa told the man, "please, if there's *any* you can spare..."

"Can't rightly say no, now can I?" the fellow said. He went back to his own car and took a siphoning hose from the trunk, slipping one end into his gas tank and the other into Grandpa's hand.

"What you'll want to do, there, is suck on that like a drinking straw." their rescuer instructed. "Once you see the gasoline's coming up, slip your end into your tank, and it'll fill her up right."

Grimacing, Grandpa popped the plastic hose in his mouth. Sucking up mouthfuls of petroleum vapor was as gross as it sounded – the taste of copper and rubbing alcohol blended together – and he popped the end of the hose into his tank moments before the vile stuff could gush in his mouth.

"That should be enough to be getting along with." the man said after a while, pinching off the flow and pulling the siphon back out.

All the Vitales gave the man their thanks, and he accepted it in good grace.

"How far away is the next town?" Grandpa asked, privately vowing to himself never, ever to let the gas in his tank fall below halfway ever again.

"Truth Or Consequences?" the man asked. "Around twenty miles down the road."

Twenty miles later, the family pulled into Truth Or Consequences, New Mexico, the only town in America to have intentionally named itself after an NBC game show. Wherever they drove, they found restaurants, streetlights, phone booths, hotels, and gas stations right alongside every inch of roadway.

Part IV

Grandpa Vitale

Mother's Father

Meet Procopio Vitale

Procopio Vitale was born in a small, pastoral village in Sicily to a large family accustomed to making ends meet. In terms of formal schooling, Grandpa never achieved more than the most rudimentary education before he stopped attending classes altogether, but he was ambitious, honest and diligent in his work—as well as gifted with an abundant wealth of common sense. Drawn by the promise of the great American Dream, Grandpa left his home and family forever to come to America.

He came to Michigan because he was fortunate enough to have an aunt and uncle there who were willing to take him in. Adjusting to life in the United States was challenging for him. He started working a number of jobs, just to get by – no task was beneath him as long as it paid the bills.

*After his marriage to Frances Leone, he went to work for his wife's family in the produce business. Gradually, he worked up enough money to build a produce store of their own—*Pete and Frank's Fruit Ranch, *which burned to the ground in a freak accident, so he rebuilt it bigger and better than before.*

Grandpa's later life has been far from uneventful. At age seventy-one, he became one of the oldest heart transplant recipients… amidst several other health concerns. Yet no matter what roadblocks were thrown in front of him, he never faltered, and treated every obstacle as a challenge to be conquered.

Quotes He Lived By

- *"It's not how much you make; it's how much you save."*
- *"A wolf may change his coat but not his habits."*
- *"You can make money by the bushel, but if you spend it by the wheelbarrow, you'll never get ahead."*
- *"People who can't get along with their family can't get along with anybody."*
- *"You have to straighten the tree out while it's young. You can't do anything if it grows up crooked."*
- *"Quitting is a small version of gutlessness."*
- *"Bad friends are like dirt in the cuff of your pants. Turn the cuff inside-out to lose the dirt."*
- *"Sometimes, in life, whether with food or other niceties, you have to skip and miss."*
- *"You have to eat a barrel of salt with someone before you really know him."*
- *"Qué será, será."*

Chapter Twenty-One

VISIONS OF PLENTY

As a young boy, Grandpa Procopio Vitale had a dream. It began with a dilapidated house deep in the countryside. Procopio knew this place well in his waking life – the house had been abandoned long before his birth, and was a frequent meeting spot for him and his friends when they went to play games – but in this dream, he came to the house alone.

Everything about the dingy home was as he remembered – creaky walls, empty doorframes, grimecrusted roof. Then his eyes fixed upon something that didn't belong: a large stone someone had apparently dropped several meters away from the cottage's front entrance, as big as a wine barrel. Acting on a sudden impulse, he rolled the rock over, until it tumbled aside. Underneath sat dirt… by all appearances, no different *that* the rest of the dirt around this old house.

Reaching into his pocket, he pulled out a spoon he'd somehow thought to bring with him from home, and knelt to dig. He was patient and methodical, but it was a long, slow undertaking. As an excavation tool, the little spoon was extremely frustrating to work with – even his bare hands would have pulled up more dirt -- yet it never occurred to him to toss it aside. He scooped and scooped, bit by bit, and when he had scraped away enough dirt to fill a wheelbarrow, the tip of the boy's spoon clinked against a metal surface. Procopio peered in to discover that he'd stumbled upon a scattered heap of coins – nothing exotic, like pirate gold, just ordinary, everyday spare change.

He stowed the money away in his pocket and resumed digging. Sure enough, more coins lay beneath the first layer. He kept on digging up money until his pockets sagged with unearthed riches. Finally satisfied, he turned from the cottage and hurried home, coins jingling all the way, crept inside his house, undressed, and slipped into bed.

Here, Procopio's magnificent dream ended. In the waking world, the boy snapped up in bed like a stepped-on rake. Flinging off his covers, he hunted through his paltry room until he'd found the pants he'd worn yesterday -- and in the dream. To his tremendous disappointment, not a single coin tumbled out, no matter how frantically he searched and shook. Completely defeated, he flung his pants down with a bitter groan.

His mother peeked in through the curtain separating her room from his. "What're you shouting for? Did you hit your head?"

"It's nothing, it's stupid… just forget about it," he answered, waving a hand dismissively. His mother would not be deterred, though, and in no time at all, Procopio found himself reluctantly relaying the details of his dream to her.

"And it was all so *vivid*!" he finished, with a glum nod towards his empty pants. "I truly believed I'd wake up and find myself rich."

His mother folded her arms – lips pursed and brows raised. "Are you certain it was a *spoon* that you dreamt… not a shovel or even a trowel?"

"No, Mama. It was definitely a spoon," he remembered.

She nodded, eyes glinting with a strange look of steely approval. "I think I understand what your dream means." she told her son. "Don't worry about money… you're going to wind up with *lots* of it. But because you used a spoon, it means you'll have to work for it – *hard.* It'll come in bits and pieces over a long, long time. But the harder you work, the more you'll earn, and if you keep at it long enough, you'll have more money than you'll ever know what to do with."

He listened to all this eagerly, smiling back brightly, sure in his heart that this was the right interpretation.

Chapter Twenty-Two

DINING ETIQUETTE

Two friends – one older, one younger – would soon be sharing a meal together in the older friend's kitchen. Two cuts of veal – one bigger, one smaller – were pulled from the older friend's icebox, dipped into olive oil, rolled over a plate of breadcrumbs, and slid into his oven. He stood by, tending the veal and steadily adding on a host of other side dishes. When all was ready, he called outside for his guest, who was rolling bocce balls with the next-door neighbor. The younger friend swung into the kitchen just as his older friend had finished setting the table. Plopping himself in a chair, he speared the larger cutlet with his fork, and dug in with relish.

Irritation simmered within the older friend, who sat watching the meat grinding through his younger friend's teeth without even taking the remaining veal off its tray.

"You're really rude, you know that?" he commented. "Here, I took all this trouble cooking this whole dinner while you played bocce… I'd think the *least* you could've done is leave me the larger piece of veal!"

The younger friend blinked at his older friend, swallowing the delicious morsel. "Well," he reasoned, "if it was you, which veal would you've picked?"

"The smaller one!" answered the older friend.

Shrugging, the younger friend sawed off another cut with his knife. "So it's just as well that I grabbed the larger piece. What're you whining about, anyway?"

Grumbling, the older friend ate his smaller veal, then moved onto the next course; a big bowl of penne pasta in a creamy pesto sauce. Both friends pulled up their spoons.

"Hey, by the way," the younger friend started up, pulling the big bowl over to himself, "I heard that your grandfather's been having health problems."

"Yeah, that's right," said the older friend. He set his spoon down, laying his forehead against the palm of his hand. "We're all very worried about him. He's suffering badly from an enlarged prostate. … Dad told me Granddad's has had a couple severe infections. He's always having to excuse himself nowadays. He cannot go an hour without having to visit the bathroom. And when he's got to go – watch out! – he runs as fast as a little boy!"

"Mmmnn," the younger friend said through his pasta, dumping in another helping.

"From what I understand, the doctors are saying that Granddad's going to need an operation – could be very expensive."

"Mmm-hmm," said the younger friend, pouring in more of the penne pasta. "What's involved?"

The older friend went on and on, elaborating the rather distasteful details of the surgery to his younger friend. From time to time a painful grimace would curdle both their faces. All throughout, the younger friend carried on eating as the older friend carried on talking.

"See what we've got to look forward to …" the older friend stopped suddenly, glancing at the empty bowl of pasta. "Did you just eat *all* of that?!"

"Yeah."

"You big glutton! Couldn't you have saved any of that for me?"

The younger friend wiped sauce from his chin with a napkin. "You could've scooped some out for yourself at any time… I wouldn't have stopped you. But you were talking so earnestly, I figured it'd be impolite to interrupt."

The older friend scowled darkly, his stomach growling audibly. "Still have room for dessert?"

"Sure do," said the younger friend, licking his spoon.

The older friend stormed back to his icebox, returning with a thick tray, of tiramisu. Again, he set the tray down at the center of the table.

"You know," the older friend started, "A friend of a friend told me *your* grandfather's not doing too well, himself."

"That's right," said the younger friend.

"So… what happened?" inquired the older friend, fingers inching towards the dessert.

"He had a heart attack and died." said the younger friend, snatching the tray before the older friend could react.

Chapter Twenty-Three

Donkey Wrangle

They claim that long ago, animals were able to talk. Records are sketchy as to when the practice of verbalizing was abandoned by most of the animal kingdom. Perhaps at some point, animals realized that their ideas and desires were more easily expressed in simple sounds – and speech as we know it fell into disuse. Even when they *could* talk, the animals were still animals. They never spent money, sang opera or performed surgery. Then, as now, they lived wild—

apart from those who lived domestically, under the attentive care of humans.

In this long-ago time, there were two villages that were linked by a treacherous mountain trail, which nobody liked to cross. Beyond the obvious hazards of avalanches and screaming plummets, this trail was also home to a very nasty band of thieves. These thieves had waylaid many a helpless traveler, some never to be seen again.

One man, who bred donkeys for a living, decided to venture across this mountain trail. He was not a brave person, but in a very desperate hurry. He selected his most able-bodied donkey, and set off, eyes peeled, staying alert to every sound and movement, while his donkey shuffled along the pebbly footpath. He'd been careful not to bring much money with him, but the donkey he was riding was worth a tidy sum.

They heard a rustle of leaves. The rider's eyes darted… was that a man's shadow, stretched out from behind that tree trunk?

"Pick up the pace." he whispered to his donkey.

"Whatever," his donkey responded, rolling his eyes with a snort.

More shadows jumped out from unlikely places when the donkey breeder chanced a look back. He thought he saw the gleam of steel as the figures pressed forward.

"Come on, come on…" he urged his donkey.

Shaking his head, the donkey trotted slightly faster. His rider twisted back again; his pursuers must've slipped out of sight.

The trail had taken them to the foot of a narrow incline, curling between a rocky mountainside and a plummeting drop.

"Down there, lads!"

The man peered upward, and spotted them at last. The robbers were standing at the top of a nearby ridge; a fierce-looking band, with wolfish features. They tossed long ropes down to the level he was riding at, and scrambled down them, hand-over-fist, with startling speed and expertise.

"Run! Now!" he shouted, shaking his donkey's reins.

The donkey drew out a long, world-weary sigh. "What for?" he asked, not increasing his pace in the slightest.

"We must go faster, or the thieves will catch us and steal you away from me!"

The donkey gave a hard swat of his tail against some intrusive flies. "So?" he replied.

The man could hardly believe this conversation. "You'd rather they capture you?"

"Makes no difference to me."

His rider balked, rather insulted now. "I feed you, I clean you, I have that barn for you out back, remember? The one that protects you from the rain and snow?"

"And I've got to carry you," the donkey reminded him, "So if someone else steals me, they've also got to feed me and clean me, and all that. It still doesn't make any difference, from where I stand."

"I've never *mistreated* you." the man quickly reminded the beast.

"I'm sure not many humans would." the donkey reasoned, "I'm a working animal, not a pet. If they abuse me… I can't carry them, plain and simple. It doesn't matter who owns me or rides me, I'm still a donkey and will be treated as such."

Not far behind them, all the robbers had finishing climbing down.

"Yes, I can understand your logic," the man told the donkey. "However," he leaned forward, whispering in the beast's long ear. "The gang of thieves who're chasing us right now are known for having a particular *fondness* for donkey meat. To them, the taste of hot, steaming donkey-kebobs are simply *irresistible*."

The donkey stiffened in dread beneath him, thought a moment, and broke into a full gallop.

Chapter Twenty-Four

The Impossible Field

It was springtime in Sicily, and the earth was finally beginning to warm on the heels of a hard winter. A young couple had just married, and as twilight blanketed the countryside, their wedding guests pushed away from their tables – faces ruddy with fine food and wine. "It is my pleasure to present my daughter and her new husband with the land that lies south of this hillside." the bride's father announced. The newlyweds flushed with gratitude as the evening air shook with congratulations.

Once their honeymoon had come and gone, the couple set out to inspect their new land. The bride packed a simple lunch of bread and sausages with some tools in a wheelbarrow, and they set out for the southern hillside. What they found made their spirits sink. No human hand had touched these fields for years, and thorny weeds had taken hold – the neglected soil lying parched and choked with rocks.

"We'll never be able to till this!" the husband exclaimed, with a sad shake of his head. "It's too much! A hundred men with a hundred horses couldn't do all this."

His bride thought a moment, appraising her groom – a tall, lean man with a boyish face, but no stranger to the demands of farm work. She drew out the blue linen tablecloth covering their picnic lunch and spread it out over the dirt.

"Could we do that much?" she asked, pointing to the square patch of blue sitting on the tawny land like a pool of cornflower sky.

"That?" he scoffed. "That little scrap is *nothing*."

So they took their shovels and set to work, breaking up the desiccated ground and turning up the soft, fresh soil lying just underneath. The husband turned to his wife – admiring her bright, dark eyes and simple beauty – and offered a smile of triumph.

His wife took up her tablecloth again – flicking her wrists so that the azure linen billowed out like a sail – and set it down again right next to the new-tilled square of land.

"How about this?" she asked.

For several hours, this process was repeated – square after square. As the sun crested over the horizon, the wife finally folded the dirty tablecloth neatly and placed it back in her basket. Exhausted and pleased, they looked at the land they had tilled stretched out at their feet in orderly, shadowed furrows. The wife turned to her husband once more.

"Can you do that much tomorrow?" she asked, with a wink.

The farmer rested his chin in his hand and thought a moment. "I can certainly try." he said at last, tipping her a smile.

Chapter Twenty-Five

Higher Education

An argument was struck by a gray-haired professor who taught zoology at the local college and a square-jawed greengrocer – both of whom had spent hours waiting in a long line for tickets to the latest hit film. The subject of contention was the old question of nature versus nurture.

"There can be no mistake!" the professor insisted, "The way in which a creature is nurtured decides their behavior."

"I'm telling you," the greengrocer snapped back, "no creature can deny its nature."

Neither of them was going to fold, and would have continued arguing for hours more… but the sun was hot, everyone's feet were sore, and the people around them had begun to pass them dirty looks.

The professor leaned in and said, "Come to my house for dinner tonight and we'll finish this debate."

"I would be delighted." the greengrocer replied evenly.

The professor smiled, and wrote his address on the back of an old receipt.

The greengrocer rang the professor's doorbell later that night, and was welcomed in with a smile both gracious and smug.

"I do hope you've brought your appetite, my friend… dinner is just coming off the stove."

The greengrocer strode inside, but amazement stopped him halfway to his seat. Sitting like sphinxes among the plates and forks were a pair of calico cats. The greengrocer had first taken them to be statues, until he saw their bellies rising and falling with air.

"Oh!" the professor said, feigning surprise, "I see you've met Socrates and Cicero. Say hello, boys."

Both felines meowed in unison, and the professor chuckled as he took a matchbook from his pocket and lit the pair of candles the cats were holding between their front paws.

"Shall we begin?" the professor asked, placing a large bowl in the center of the table. Whatever else, the professor was a good cook, and no miser with his food.

"So," the professor prompted smugly, "tell me more about your outlook on animals not being able to overcome their basic natures."

"How did you train them like this?" the greengrocer asked, petting Socrates, but getting no reaction from the cat.

"It wasn't easy," the professor bragged, launching into an overly detailed explanation involving a lot of college-level words the greengrocer had never heard before.

The greengrocer's attention kept returning to the calicos. The candles they held were made of a natural beeswax, and it was disconcerting to watch the hot, translucent beads dribble down between the pink pads of their paws.

"Doesn't the wax hurt them?" the greengrocer asked.

"They're used to it." the professor assured him, pouring a third glass of wine.

To their credit, Socrates and Cicero held themselves with the poise of yoga masters, even as their paws were gloved in paraffin. Finally, when the candles had burned low enough to almost singe the cats' whiskers, the professor extinguished the flames with a brass snuffer.

"Scat!" he commanded, and the calicos dashed off the table and out of the room. "You see?" the professor cried, thumping the table victoriously, "Nurturing wins!"

"Could I come by your house tomorrow night?" the greengrocer asked, "I'd like to bring my friends, and show them these remarkable cats of yours!"

"By all means!" the professor said, beaming.

The following night, the professor opened his door to find a whole crowd of people gathered on his porch – the butcher, the baker, the health inspector, the stockbroker, the district attorney… and of course, who could forget the accordion repairman?

"My goodness!" the professor exclaimed, showing them in, "You're practically a traveling circus!"

Socrates and Cicero were already in place on the tabletop, fresh candles clutched in their paws. The greengrocer waited, letting his friends marvel at the cats.

"I honestly don't know if I have enough food for you all!" the professor crowed.

"You know, I think it's a real shame, professor." the greengrocer said at last, "All this food for us, while the real stars of the show go hungry. Here!"

He pulled a bag from inside his coat pocket, pulled it open, and spilled a pair of mice onto the table. The moment they saw the rodents sniffing about the plates, the calicos dropped their candles and scampered after them. Over the tumultuous din that ensued, the greengrocer pointed at the sullen professor, and said, "You see, sir… nature wins!"

Chapter Twenty-Six

Fava Beans

A new monk had just been inducted into a monastic brotherhood. To celebrate, all the monks in the order threw what was for them, at least, a grand banquet, indeed: bowls and bowls of spaghetti with a nice, healthy serving of fresh-baked fava beans mixed in for flavor. Joyous as the moment was, the abbot who presided over this monastery could not help observing how little his new charge was partaking in the feast. Even as the man chatted and laughed with the other brothers, he only picked at individual strands of linguini with barely disguised looks of remorse. Though his colleagues helped themselves freely to seconds, thirds, and fourths, the man of the hour hadn't eaten a quarter-ways through his first bowl.

"Does something trouble you, brother?" the abbot asked. "You've scarcely touched your meal. Pray tell, what has stolen your appetite?"

The new monk smiled up at him. "Nothing to worry about, father! I celebrated with my own family just this afternoon, and I've had my fill."

The abbot folded his hands and said no more about it that evening.

The next morning, the new monk sought out the head cook. "Listen," he said with a friendly smile, "from now on, never serve me fava beans."

"Why? Are you allergic?" the cook asked.

"No," the new monk admitted, "I just despise them. Feed them to someone who can stomach them, but don't bother putting any more on my plate." he said, leaving to tend the tomatoes in the monastery garden. Later that same morning, the new monk was approached by the abbot.

"Our head cook tells me you won't eat fava beans."

"That's right, father." the monk confirmed.

The abbot hung his head in disappointment. "Brother," he said softly, "I believe a small measure of quiet seclusion might be prudent. Perhaps some time for personal introspection and private meditation would help you see things in a different light."

The new monk swallowed hard, but had to capitulate. "If you think it best, father." he agreed, bowing.

An hour later, the new monk was brought to a small, freshly-swept alcove. Slightly more spacious than a standard prison cell, the room contained a bed, a bookshelf with a Bible on it, a chamber pot, and a carved crucifix on the wall. The door itself had a large hatch that slid open and shut from the outside.

"You will remain here for a week." the abbot told him. "Use this opportunity for meditation and prayer. If you feel agitated or cramped, simply rap on the door and we'll let you out."

The new monk nodded gloomily – knowing that if he were to demand release before his week of penance was fully served, he might as well turn in his robes and rosary and go back to tending mules.

"God keep you." the abbot bade, bolting the door behind him.

More than a little incensed, the new monk grabbed the Bible and slumped on the bed, rereading his favorite Old Testament passages. Why was it *his* fault the Lord had given him taste buds which curdled at the flavor of fava beans? When the monastery bells struck noon, the head cook slid open the hatch, handing the new monk a slice of bread and cup of water. Seven hours later, he returned with fresh water and bread, and so it went for several days.

The new monk remained sequestered in the alcove, each meal enough to sustain him, but not *satisfy* him. He would listen to the shuffle of other monks passing his cloister, and reminisce longingly about the fabulous bounty of spaghetti he had turned down on his first day. On the fourth day, the new monk was pacing his room restlessly, trying to distract his petulant stomach. He looked up towards the ceiling, meaning to beg God for guidance…

What he saw gave him pause. A squat iron chandelier hung from a hook, and from the chandelier hung a bag. The new monk could see the end of it dangling off the side, lumpy with *something*. Had it always been there? He felt a bit embarrassed to not have noticed it before, having always prayed towards the crucifix on the wall.

He stretched for the bag, but it was too high up. So he pulled his bed over and stood on top of it, but it was *still* out of reach. Finally, he removed one of his sandals, swung back, and was just able to swipe the bottom of the bag's dangling end. Eagerly he struck at the bag again and again… and eventually, he was able to scratch open a hole in the fabric. At first, he couldn't tell what treasure was spilling out the bag —small and hard as coat buttons, they rattled on the stone of the floor like winter hail. He jumped from his bed, picked one up, and placed it in his mouth. *Fava beans*.

The rest of the brotherhood entered, drawn by the clatter. When they opened the door, they found the new monk gobbling up the riches which had rained down on him – not caring that they weren't soft and baked, but raw and hard as seashells, grinning like a kid facing a table of birthday presents.

Up stepped the abbot, staring down with a slight smile. "How are your beans?"

"*Delicious*," said the new monk, and meant it.

Chapter Twenty-Seven

Pete & Frank's

Procopio Vitale was the 'Pete' of *Pete & Frank's Fruit Ranch*. He had adopted this nickname so friends and customers wouldn't have to stumble through the pronunciation of 'Procopio.' The 'Frank' was one Frank Orlando, Pete's business partner. The store they'd pinned their names and fortunes on sat along the intersection of 9 Mile and Kelly in Eastpointe, Michigan – a quiet, conventional community of brick houses and wide, paved roads.

Pete & Frank's

The two men had started selling Christmas trees in 1959, and made enough to set up a garden supply shop the following year. The shopkeepers barely made ends meet selling flowerpots and bushels of dirt, and for two years a 'FOR SALE' sign hung in *Pete & Frank's* front window—in case some other ambitious entrepreneur wished to try his luck. Their story could very easily have ended there when just such a fellow made Pete and Frank an offer for their building.

The contract was drawn, and the buyer's signature had joined Frank Orlando's on the final page when the document was passed to Pete Vitale. His pen almost touched the paper, then he sat back.

"Very sorry for wasting your time, sir," Pete said, tearing the document down the middle in front of the astonished men, "but I've decided I'm keeping my store after all."

Having thrown their hats into the proverbial ring, the partners re-evaluated themselves. They turned *Pete & Frank's* into a combination produce store and garden center. As 1963 drew to a close, the bills were all paid with enough left over for Pete and Frank to stow in their bank accounts. For half a decade, the partners did progressively better—making sales and attracting a loyal following of customers.

By 1968, the store had grown into a full-fledged produce market, selling vegetables, fruit, milk, bread and packaged goods. Frank Orlando and Pete Vitale had been business partners for nearly nine years—managing a thriving, well-regarded shop with the help of their families and a small army of part-time, teen-age workers.

Quite suddenly, Frank Orlando's mind turned towards other pursuits.

"The produce business has been good to us, Pete, but I'm not sure I can stick with it to the end of my days." he confessed one evening, as they were shutting off the lights to go home. "I'm thinking of maybe doing something on my own. My heart's not set on anything yet, one way or another, but I'm considering my options."

Frank Orlando had always been restless like this. Before meeting Pete, Frank had been a construction worker, dabbled in the hardware business, and had even been a serviceman for the U.S. Army. He was in his forties now, but as solid as his finances were, Frank was still certain there'd be something better someplace else.

Pete said nothing at first. As they strolled down

the parking lot towards their garage, he straightened and said, "You know, Frank, I've been thinking about taking a trip to Italy. A little vacation, maybe a couple of weeks."

"Well, you've certainly earned it." Frank said, with a laugh of surprise. Vacations had to be more or less forced upon Pete Vitale – and this was the first time in their nine-year partnership that he'd volunteered for one.

"I'd like my wife to see Italy," Pete sighed, "and I've been meaning to see my brother, Santo, again."

Frank had heard the story. Pete had left his whole family behind in Sicily to come to the United States. Both his parents had passed away since he left, but his brother, Santo, was still in the old country.

"Good," said Frank, "you go enjoy Italy and when you come back, I'll take a vacation of my own, then we'll discuss what we're going to do with the store."

Everything was ready the weekend before Pete's trip was scheduled. The passports were at hand, the plane tickets had been bought and the suitcases were packed. As thrilling as it all was, Pete hadn't let his excitement overshadow his duties as store manager – if anything, his efforts had redoubled. In the weeks leading up to his departure he settled matters so that when he returned from Italy, he'd find the store better than when he'd left it.

"Accounts differ, regarding the source of the spark which set things in motion that fateful night, on the 23rd of July. Some remember the vicious thunderstorm that had been churning over the store the night before, and blame it. Others fault a smoker's stray cigarette, flicked carelessly close to some empty cardboard boxes, and then forgotten. Whatever the case, when it happened everyone had already gone to bed. And as they all slept peacefully, it continued through the night, unseen and unrestrained, taking on a life of its own."

Pete Vitale was facing his mirror in the early morning, scraping his cheeks with a razor when he got the call.

"Am I speaking to Mr. Pete Vitale?" a brusque-sounding fellow asked over the phone.

"Yes, you are." Pete said, having hustled into his kitchen to take the call.

"This is the Eastpointe Fire Department," said the caller, "We tried calling your partner, Mr. Orlando, but were unable to reach him."

"Is something the matter, sir?" Pete asked, concentration sharpening with his voice.

"It's your store, Mr. Vitale. We're dealing with a little fire that broke out at your store last night."

"A little fire?" Pete repeated. "I'll be right over."

It wasn't until he saw columns of ash and smoke billowing into the sky, a mile's distance from his store that Pete could appreciate what an enormous understatement he'd been told. Scores of firefighters from six separate communities were deluging the building with water from every available hydrant. 9 Mile and Kelly roads both had to be completely closed off.

Days later, the inspectors would uncover the specific cause of the fire's inextinguishable power. *Pete & Frank's* had had a series of industrial heaters suspended from its ceiling. As the conflagration had really built high, the heaters all broke, rupturing the gas pipes inside them, so that for all the water the firemen turned on *Pete & Frank's*, the blaze was being nurtured by a steady reservoir of flammable gas from within.

The forces of man and flame were locked in stalemate, and it was all the firefighters could do to keep the fires from spreading out to neighboring buildings. Hours crawled by, and Pete and Frank and both their families could only watch in dismay. When the firemen finally deduced that something had to be wrong with the gas, they phoned the gas company over. But there was a problem; the valve controlling *Pete & Frank's* gas flow had rusted in place from complete disuse, so that even with their strongest tools, the gas people *could not shut the valve*. The inferno finally died only when they physically cinched the gas pipe shut.

Later, the Vitale and Orlando families were allowed to examine what remained of *Pete & Frank's*. It looked like a war had torn through it. Almost everything was ashen and charred; the stench of smoke here was thick and foul. Water from all the firefighting was pooled up at their feet and in the display cases, and slathered over every flat surface. Every bit of equipment, from the plumbing to their garbage incinerator, was beyond repair. Though the coolers had survived the conflagration fairly well, their contents had been spoiled by smoke damage.

The produce that had survived the blaze was thoroughly ruined – the watermelons in particular were as hot as baked potatoes, and when they cracked open they leaked a sickly-sweet soup. All the dollars in the office drawers were little more than bundles of blackened leaves that crumpled at the slightest touch. The coins had liquefied together into shapeless masses of copper, nickel and silver slag.

While everyone was thankful that no one had been injured or killed by the fire, and their parking lot and garage had escaped incineration, inspectors from the Board of Health popped in and condemned the building.

"If you want to rebuild on this site," Frank and Pete were informed, "all this has to be cleared away first."

"What're we going to do?" Frank moaned later, as they sat morosely together in their truck.

"We rebuild." Pete stated, rubbing his tired eyes as he sat up straighter.

The next morning, Pete cancelled his plane tickets and phoned his brother, Santo, to deliver the bad news.

"No worries, Procopio," Santo assured his brother in their native Italian, "You go do what you need to, as you always have."

The next step was collecting on their insurance, but Frank Orlando had never had any real faith in the concept of insurance.

"If anything needs repairing," he'd often said with a smile, "I can fix it with my own two hands." The small policy he had purchased was more to humor his business partner than act as a safeguard against catastrophes he was positive would never occur. When the insurance agents calculated the damages, the best they could offer was $49,000 for the building and $17,000 for the contents—chump change.

They had to clear away the debris and begin building a new store, but construction would take months, and they needed a source of income in the meanwhile.

"You know what?" Pete told Frank, "We should go get a tent."

His partner brightened at this idea, but suggested they clear it with Uncle Sam's boys, just to cover their bases. So the two men went to get permission from the city of Eastpointe. Most of the government officials they spoke to had no problems allowing them permission to sell from a tent, but the Board of Health had a complaint.

"As food-handlers, your employees must have access to at least one restroom fully furnished with running water." they told Pete and Frank. The partners had enough in their budget to afford a little electricity, but indoor plumbing would be another matter.

DJ's Playboy Party Store — a neighbor who'd benefited from *Pete and Frank's* presence — was happy to help Pete and Frank out in their time of need. The party store's owners wrote a letter giving the staff of Pete & Frank's permission to use their bathrooms. Thankfully, the Board of Health considered this an adequate solution.

So Pete and Frank rented a massive, red and white striped tent and set it up in their parking lot. They put up some tables, installed a few lights and counted on the hard work and patience of their families. Their choice of stock was limited. They had to restrict themselves to produce like apples, oranges, zucchini and cabbage that wouldn't spoil outdoors.

For all that Pete Vitale had lost to the fire, he still retained one precious commodity—his reputation. Because of the good name he'd made for himself over years of solid business, several of his old suppliers were willing to let him and Frank continue selling their produce on a line of good credit, and faithful customers continued buying from them.

It was seven o'clock at night, about seven days after they'd started selling from the rented tent. A storm had been brewing overhead, turbulently fierce… rather like the storm that'd heralded the fire, a little over a week ago. The storm was a furious, savage thing, a riot of lightning flares, pelting rainfall and gusting wind. Pete and Frank and their wives and children rushed to move everything from the tent into the garage.

One of the Orlando children pointed upwards, where rain was dribbling in through a gash at the top of the tent. And then the wind picked up – the type of surging, piercing gust that sailors dread – catching in the gash and ripping straight through its whole roof like a dull knife mangling an envelope. Rain pounded on hurrying heads and the wind scattered loose fruits as Pete shouted encouragement and ran with armfuls of produce until he caught sight of his partner.

Frank Orlando stood stock-still in the downpour, glaring skyward with a look of heartbroken disgust.

Why me?! Frank's face clearly asked. *Why now?! What next?!*

"Frank!" Pete yelled.

But his partner just kept staring up, waiting for God to explain.

• • •

Frank Orlando was beside himself with frustration.

"That's *it*," he told Pete, shivering with rage and cold as the last box was loaded into the garage. "I can recognize a sign from above when I see one. The store's been jinxed, my friend. We need to quit."

Pete could hardly blame his partner for having reached his limit. Frank Orlando had entered the produce business knowing nothing, and had learned everything he knew about managing a produce store on the fly.

"Okay, Frank," Pete agreed, gently, "Tomorrow we'll clean up that mess," he gestured at the wrecked tent, "and that'll be that."

At eight o'clock the next morning, Frank Orlando pulled into their parking lot to find his partner setting out merchandise beneath the battered tent. "They told me you were crazy," he stated, slamming his car door. "Now I know. Pete, we agreed we were going to quit!"

"Well, what can I tell you?" Pete responded, wiping his brow with the underside of his arm. "You want to quit? Go home and God bless you. As for me, when I've got no more strength, no more breath, then I stop." Throwing up his hands, Frank shuffled over wearily to help his partner unload boxes.

Pete had the tent repaired, and Frank converted the garage into a cooler so that their merchandise would stay fresher, longer. Week by week, sales rose and construction on the new *Pete & Frank's* building proceeded. By the end of November, they closed down the tent. Construction was still incomplete, but they knew the produce would only freeze if left outside. A construction crew was already doing the brunt of the building, but the grocers were more than willing to lend them a hand. Frank Orlando was pouring cement one afternoon when a sharp, biting pain sprung up in his chest. He groaned and clutched his ribcage. Mrs. Orlando came and picked Frank up and drove her husband to the local hospital, where he had a mild heart attack.

Although Frank Orlando was only in his forties, the stress of all that had followed the brutal fire had decimated his heart. His physicians informed him that he was only fit to work five hours a day, at a low-pressure job. At the end of January of 1969, he came to Pete.

"I can't work with you anymore, Pete," he said, drained and fatigued. "Either buy me out, or I'll buy you out, or we'll sell out together."

"I'll buy you out." Pete offered. The two men got an appraisal, split up the money they had between them, and wished each other the best of luck. With that, the partners parted ways.

• • •

In the late 1940's, a young man named Procopio Vitale left his Sicilian village of Cinisi to seek his fortune in the United States. Keeping true to his young dream, he established *Pete & Frank's Fruit Ranch* in 1959, cultivating a thriving business for himself, only to watch all the fruits of his labor go up in smoke in the summer of 1968. After buying out Frank Orlando, he threw himself completely into the rebirth of his store – marketing his produce as though nothing else was left for him in the world, and he did it alone.

Now, it was the summer of 1973, the young man's fortunes had grown bigger than he'd ever hoped, and he was home at last.

He stepped off the plane with his wife and three daughters – his three sons were all grown up now, and managing *Pete & Frank's* for him back in Michigan.

"Procopio!" called a voice, as they stepped out from the plane at the gate. There stood Santo Vitale, his beloved older brother. He couldn't believe how old he'd grown after nearly twenty-five years.

The brothers hugged each other fiercely, and then Pete turned and introduced his daughters. The Vitale girls all understood some Italian, but still smiled uncertainly when Santo welcomed them to Italy.

"That store of yours… is it doing well without you?" Santo asked.

"I wouldn't have flown out here if it weren't." Pete Vitale said. "I'm sorry it took this long for me to return."

Santo shook his head. "Really, Procopio, I'm amazed to see you back here this *quickly*, considering all you've been through."

The new *Pete & Frank's* was genuinely successful. Many of their customers didn't even remember the original store, insisting, "I remember you when you first started out, in that tent!"

How had he done it? The answer is nothing more grand or humble than hard work and perseverance. Quitting was not part of Pete Vitale.

Chapter Twenty-Eight

The Future's Not Ours to See

No one had any idea all was not well with Grandpa Vitale's heart, back in 1992. He was closed-lipped – even with his family – quietly swallowing his daily medications and carrying on with his life. Prescription pills wouldn't provide Grandpa a permanent solution, and by the spring of 1999, Grandpa Vitale found himself breathless and weary most all of the time.

On May 14th, Grandpa was cracking jokes with two of my uncles at his produce store, when he fell faint in the middle of the vegetable aisle. A dead weight was clamping down on his chest like a vise, and my uncles rushed him into the backroom, intending to call an ambulance.

"No ambulance!" Grandpa gasped, throwing my Uncle Dave the keys to his own car. "There's no time, drive me to the hospital!"

They wheeled him straight over to the intensive care ward, where the doctors jolted him with electricity until his irregular heart rate had normalized.

On May 15th, Grandpa had his seventy-first birthday. He woke in one of the hospital beds, surrounded by his family – they'd all dropped everything they'd been doing when they learned what'd happened. He reassured everyone that he was feeling somewhat better now, and unwrapped the presents they'd brought. A nurse called them out after a while, so that a doctor could come in.

"Happy birthday, Mr. Vitale," the doctor said, shaking his head with a grin. "I've actually given you a present of my own. It's hidden in a very special place – you'll never guess where."

"Where?" Grandpa asked.

The doctor pulled back some of Grandpa's hospital gown.

"Right inside your chest," said the doctor, tapping gently upon a new scar. "A nifty little gizmo called a 'defibrillator.'"

The doctor explained to Grandpa that his heart had grown abnormally enormous, to the point where it could hardly pump his blood at all. Grandpa's new defibrillator was programmed to keep track of his heartbeats. If his heart slowed down again, the defibrillator would give it a shock to re-stabilize him.

"It'll be like having me right next to you all day, every day!" the cardiologist chuckled.

From there, it wasn't long at all before Grandpa Vitale had reached a stage of abject misery. While the cardiologist's gift prevented him from dying outright, it couldn't stop his body from growing progressively sicker and weaker. Doctors tried to help by rewiring his defibrillator and even installing an experimental pacemaker—but Grandpa's health kept spiraling relentlessly downward, until he was more frail and helpless than he'd ever been. He couldn't work. He couldn't go outside. The simple act of rising from his armchair and walking the few feet to his bedroom exhausted him completely. Family members had to help him in and out of bed, clothes, cars, chairs and showers. His doctors warned that he probably wouldn't make it through to the year 2000 millennium.

"I may be alive," Grandpa said, at last, "but I'm sure not living. There has to be another way!"

At this point, my father—Bob Badalament—intervened. Dad wasn't a cardiologist, but as a medical professional he knew that Grandpa's only hope was a heart transplant, and he knew a patient who had survived one. This fellow was happy to pay Grandpa a visit and point him in the right direction.

"A heart transplant is risky, you may even die," the patient admitted, "but it's meant the difference between really *living* and just staying alive."

Grandpa agreed.

The cost of a new heart was nothing short of astronomical, and the precious organs were not doled out frivolously. The doctors at Cleveland Clinic wouldn't even consider Grandpa; he was far too old to waste a heart on. The same thing happened at the University of Michigan.

"Look at it from our side," Grandpa was told, "If

you had just one single heart to offer, would you give it to a younger patient with twenty-five more years, or an older one with about ten years, at best?"

Then one of the cardiologists suggested they check the University of Cincinnati; he had a colleague who wouldn't reject Grandpa outright on his age. So Mom helped Grandpa and Grandma into her car, and drove them from Michigan to Ohio. When Grandpa entered the University of Cincinnati, he sat down for a meal and went into heart failure. The doctors had no choice but to admit him as a patient.

"Please consider him for a heart transplant." my mother and grandmother begged.

They agreed to assess Grandpa Vitale, but couldn't promise he'd qualify for their list.

So began the tests. They needed his A+ blood type on record, because a heart of a different blood type would be rejected by Grandpa's system. They reviewed Grandpa's medical history, all the way back to his parents in Italy. They tested for whether he smoked, drank, or took drugs. They analyzed Grandpa for other illnesses, (because if he'd had cancer on top of a bad heart, he wouldn't even be in the running.)

Grandpa passed the physical examinations with

flying colors.

Still, the doctors were really and truly against allowing Grandpa a new heart – he was just so very *old*. So they brought Grandpa, Mom, and Grandma for a talk, to learn about Grandpa as a person, and determine the measure of his character;

"How long have you been married for, Mr. Vitale?"

"How close are you with your wife? Were there any earlier marriages?"

"Any kids, Mr. Vitale? How many?"

"Do you see your kids often?"

When the doctors were finished talking with him, they turned to Grandma and my Mom, to get his family's assessment.

"How would you characterize your father's temperament?"

"Has he been compliant as a patient?"

"What is his personal history like?"

My mother was quite happy to share her father's past. She explained Grandpa's habit of always meeting adversity head-on – from his immigration to America, to the huge family he'd raised. How he'd found the challenge in the long chain of jobs he'd held before building *Pete & Frank's*. Listening along from his chair, Grandpa smiled tenderly as his daughter described the string of hardships he'd soldiered through after *Pete & Frank's* had burned to the ground, never quitting where others would.

Grandpa's fortitude amazed the doctors. Certainly, they hadn't seen a stalwart, resolute warrior when Grandpa first walked into their hospital. Now they recognized the hallmarks of an ideal patient: flexible, cooperative, and uncomplaining – the type who'd wage a good fight for his life.

"Chronologically, he may be seventy-one," one of them commented, "But before his heart troubles, he was functioning like a much younger person." So they gave him a place in their hospital, and wrote his name on their transplant list.

In its own right, this phase was even rougher for Grandpa than overcoming the medical community's reluctance. Hearts weren't simply withdrawn from blood banks, after all. Vital organs, like lobsters, worked best at their absolute freshest. Only volunteers could donate hearts for transplants – and blood types had to match exactly. Moreover, names that were higher up on the list had seniority over Grandpa.

Each agonizing day was like waiting for the world's slowest slot machine to churn out matching fruit. Patients had died waiting. One fellow – with a rare blood type and suffering from *situs inversus* – had been waiting here since last year. For a while, there just weren't any hearts coming in. Grandpa could only hold tough and swallow down the hospital's Jell-O and runny soups.

"You should go home to Michigan," Grandma urged my mother, adding, "Is Carey, Ohio too far out of your way?" Carey, Ohio was home to the National Shrine Of Our Lady of Consolation, a special church renowned for its miracles.

"No," my mother said, "it's not too far."

"Stop there and light a candle on your way home." Grandma said.

Sometime around then, things started turning around. Several times over the next few weeks, the University of Cincinnati would receive a new heart, and with each transplant the cardiologists performed, Grandpa Vitale moved one name closer to the top of the transplant list.

• • •

It was 10:00 the night we got the call. I was a high school senior. It was early for me to be slipping in bed, but a test was scheduled the following morning and I wanted to be well-rested. My brother, Peter, lay in his bed on the other side of the room. The thin, bright numbers of my digital clock were the only light. I was not yet asleep.

Our phone rang, and my parents answered it, from across the hall in their bedroom. Then came a shrill, piercing "WHAT?!" from my mother. My brother and I both jerked up in bed, as Mom dashed to our doorway, her hand tight around a cordless phone.

"They've found him a heart!" she said, breathlessly. "Get dressed… I want you two and Grace in the car in ten minutes!"

In all honesty, it was amazing we didn't get into a traffic accident. Whatever the speed limit was, Dad matched it—exceeding it whenever police presence looked thin. Stopping only once, for an uncle who wanted to come along, we made it to the hospital in Cincinnati minutes before his operation.

My grandfather looked as if some heartless monster had hooked him up to a machine and pumped all the liquid and muscle from his tired frame. This was truly the verge of death I was seeing. He lay on a gurney—bristling with tubes, his body pallid and feeble but his face shining with such love and warmth that we felt blessed by his gentle smile. We each kissed him, one by one.

"Are you alright, Grandpa?" I asked.

Of us all, this whole ordeal had been hardest on my Mom. She looked ready to cry. My mother asked, "Dad, are you afraid? Are you nervous?"

He looked back, very strong, very determined.

"If I come out on the other side, it's gonna be okay," he told us all. "If not, that's it."

Just before the nurses rolled the gurney towards the operating room, he murmured, "*Qué será, será.*"

All of us, Grandpa included, knew he might not come through. If so, this was his message we were to pass on to everyone else who couldn't be with us tonight.

What words to leave your life with… what words to live your life by! There was nothing to do but huddle together in the waiting room with Grandma. The adults clung to their cell phones, updating the rest of the family of Grandpa's condition. We pushed the rows of waiting room chairs together to form makeshift cots and slept fitfully. With the dawn, a television above us began playing old soap opera reruns—devious affairs where no one ever laughed or brawled. The magazines traded in gossip, parenting, architecture and gardening.

"I think Grandpa's going to make it," my brother Peter said, confidently.

"He's made it this far," my father replied. "It's in God's hands now."

When his doctor emerged, we all gathered around.

"The surgery's gone well," he announced.

It was thrilling. We thanked God and the team of doctors that'd pulled Grandpa through.

"Mr. Vitale still has a long road of recovery ahead," the doctor cautioned at last. "A new heart takes quite some time for a body to adjust to – he still runs the risk of rejection."

We nodded and listened. We could deal with it.

There'd always be an 'it,' and win or lose, we could handle whatever 'it' was.

As Doris Day had sung in that sweet old song, and as so many everyday Italian men had said to the great fog of uncertainty life always threw up in their faces;

Whatever will be, will be.

GRANDSON'S FAREWELL

Whew!

I'm parched! Let me just grab myself a sip of water, here. Storytelling gets to be thirsty work, after all… Great Scott… would you look at the time! How long have we been at this? I'd probably better stop here. Oh, don't get me wrong, I do have a whole bunch more stories to share… but this is definitely enough for one sitting, I think. I wouldn't want to hold you up from your other commitments, after all.

You've been such a terrific guest to have over. I really hope you enjoyed listening to all my grandparents' old tales, because I certainly had a whole lot of fun telling them. Let me take that plate and cup off your hands, and put them in the sink. Again, thank you so much for staying as long as you have, it really means a lot to me. And listen… if you're interested, we could probably check our schedules and maybe arrange another get-together.

Take care!

Pronunciation Guide

Badalament *is a four-syllable name:*

1) *Buh* as in '*butter*'
2) *Dal* as in '*Dallas*'
3) *Luh* as in '*luggage*'
4) *Meant* as in 'I *meant* to do that.'

Put them all together and you get 'Buh-dal-luh-meant!'

Vitale *is a three-syllable name:*

1) *Vi* as in '*vitamin*'
2) *Tally* as in '*Tally* up their scores.'

Put them together and you get 'Vi-tally!'

Procopio *is a four-syllable name:*

1) *Pro* as in '*produce*'
2) C*o* as in 'c*ode*'
3) *Pi* as in '*piano*'
4) O as in 'O, for a muse of fire!"

Put them together and you get 'Pro-co-pi-o!'

Cinisi *is a three-syllable name:*

1) *She* as in '*sheep*'
2) *Nuh* as in '*nugget*'
3) *Zee* as in '*zebra*'

Put them together and you get 'She-nuh-zee!'

Picture Appendix

Page 5: My parents, Robert and Providence Badalament.

Page 15: My grandmother, Grace Badalament, at age 7.

Page 24: My great-grandmother, Grace Costello, and my grandmother, Grace Badalament, at age 14.

Page 27: My grandmother, Grace Badalament, at age 11, dancing at an MGM studio set.

Page 36: My grandmother, Grace Badalament, age 17.

Page 43: My grandmother, Grace Badalament, age 13.

Page 49: My great-grandmother, Grace Costello, as a cashier at my great-uncle Sam Costello's family market, circa mid-1960s.

Page 61: My great-grandfather, Anthony Badalament with his three sons, Peter (standing), Louis (my grandfather, seated left), and Joseph (seated right), circa 1925.

Page 69: My great-grandparents, Anthony and Rose Badalament, circa late 1936.

Page 72: From left to right, my grandfather, Louis Badalament (wearing cap), his neighbor, Joe Fitzgerald, and my great-uncle Joseph Badalament, circa 1932.

Page 77: My grandfather, Louis Badalament, age 83.

Page 82: My grandfather, Louis Badalament, and my father, Robert Badalament, circa 1990.

Page 86: My uncle and godfather, Michael Badalament, in 1969.

Page 91: My uncle, Stephen Badalament, circa 1999.

Page 101: From left to right: my mother, Providence Badalament, myself, my grandmother, Frances Vitale, and my brother, Peter Badalament, circa 1991.

Page 106: My grandmother, Frances Vitale, and my great-grandmother, Providenza Leone, circa 1947.

Page 112: My grandmother, Frances Vitale, at age 17.

Page 117: My grandmother, Frances Vitale, at age 18.

Page 122: My grandparents, Peter and Frances Vitale, and my uncles, Vito Vitale (right rear), Peter Vitale (left front), and Frank Vitale (right front), circa 1958.

Page 129: My great-grandfather, Vito Leone (in foreground), with friends, circa early 1940s.

Page 136: From left to right: my uncle, Peter Vitale, my grandmother, Frances Vitale, my aunt, Lisa Vitale, my mother, Providence Vitale Badalament, my uncle, Frank Vitale, and my grandfather, Pete Vitale, circa 1967.

Page 149: My great-grandmother, Lisa Vitale, circa late 1950s.

Page 153: From left to right: my grandfathers Louis Badalament and Pete Vitale, in 1997.

Page 158: My grandfather, Pete Vitale, and my mother, Providence Badalament, 1965.

Page 163: My grandparents, Frances and Pete Vitale, on their wedding day, November 10, 1951.

Page 166: My grandfather, Pete Vitale, at his fish market, circa 1953.

Page 171: My grandfather, Pete Vitale, circa 1950.

Page 176: My grandparents Frances and Pete Vitale, on the day of Pete and Frank's Fruit Ranch reopening, 1970.

Page 191: My grandfather, Pete Vitale, recovering from his heart transplant, October 1999.

Page 210: Louis Badalament, II, (myself), age 7.

About The Author

Louis Francis Badalament, II is a graduate of Ohio University's Scripps School of Journalism and Vancouver Film School's scriptwriting program. His lifelong passion is writing and storytelling in all mediums, including film, literature, and the performing arts. Currently, he's working on his first graphic novel, *Maglenda's Errand-Girls*, scheduled for release in 2010 by Alterna Comics. Louis lives in Michigan, within traveling distance of all four of his grandparents.

Buying Additional Copies Of This Book

If you're interested in purchasing more copies of *Tales I Grew Up With: The Grandparents*, please contact us at:

Badalament Ink

1202 Walton Boulevard, Suite #211

Rochester Hills, MI 48307-6900

Or visit our website at www.badalamentink.com.